Fair Game

Dewey rode up to the front porch and dismounted, breaking the spell that seemed to have been cast over Harrison Powell's assembled guests.

Dr. Lisa Nelson stood straight and looked around at the hunting party. "I'm afraid nothing can be done for him."

Dewey approached the group.

"Harrison Powell," someone said. "He's dead."

Dr. Nelson was a young woman, but she radiated competence. "I think we'd better just come clean now. Who fired the shot?"

Everyone looked stunned. Finally Sonny Royce spoke. "There seems to be a problem about that."

"What do you mean, a problem?" asked Dr. Nelson.

Royce scratched his beard and took a deep breath. "Lisa, listen. It wasn't one of us."

A DEWEY JAMES MYSTERY

MYSTERY LOVES COMPANY

KATE MORGAN

BERKLEY BOOKS, NEW YORK

MYSTERY LOVES COMPANY

A Berkley Book / published by arrangement with
the author

PRINTING HISTORY
Berkley edition / April 1992

ISBN: 0-425-13237-4

**For Sarah Boone,
our new friend**

1

"PARDON ME," SAID the young man on the street corner, leaning down to tap at the window of a dusty old station wagon. He looked inquiringly at the driver and smiled.

The bright-eyed, silver-haired woman behind the wheel was full of curiosity. Obligingly she rolled down her window and inspected the stranger. He was tall, blond, blue-eyed; well formed and graceful—handsome in a deceivingly casual way, his good looks somehow enhanced by his disheveled hair, worn jeans, and tatty leather jacket. Behind gold-rimmed spectacles his eyes shone with humor and intelligence. He could have been a model for rugged outdoor wear, thought the woman. In all her sixty-odd years, she had never encountered so perfect a young man on the sleepy sidewalks of Hamilton. He looked almost too good to be true.

"Yes?" she asked.

"Could you tell me the way to the rectory?"

"Good Shepherd? Or All Angels?" The rectory! What on earth did this fellow want at the rectory?

"I don't know the name of the church, I'm afraid. But I'm looking for a man called Cedric Hastings."

"Oh—Cedric. Well. Yes, you go out about a mile and a half—out Howard Street, turn right when you reach Sherman, and then left on High. Number Four." She glanced toward the back seat, where Isaiah, a large and faithful black Labrador retriever, regarded the stranger with a mixture of distrust and hopefulness. In Isaiah's mind, she knew, there was always the possibility that a stranger brought treats. But he was a fairly good watchdog when no treats were forthcoming. She looked carefully at the man and decided to risk it.

"Can I give you a lift? I'm going that way."

"Thanks. I'll take you up on it." He smiled and swung his knapsack off his shoulders.

They set off through the scant late-afternoon traffic on Howard Street. "I take it you are a friend of Cedric's?" she asked as the young man slouched comfortably in the front seat.

Cedric Hastings had been rector of the Church of the Good Shepherd for more than forty years. He was an unusual man; an odd mixture of practicality and spirituality, with a passion for thrift, the literature of ancient Greece, and the theology of Saint Anselm. His sermons were often a trifle erudite for the good people of his congregation; but he didn't allow the limits of their schooling to deter him from preaching at an intensely intellectual level. Some of his flock suspected Cedric of wishing to educate them.

"In a way. My name is Harrison Powell."

"And mine is Dewey James. What brings you to Hamilton, Mr. Powell?"

"Ancient history. I came to look Cedric up—he worked with my father, a long time ago."

"Oh—your father is a clergyman?" Dewey asked. This was unexpected. She looked at the young man more intently.

"Was. He's been dead about a year now—but Dad and Cedric were missionaries together in Africa somewhere."

"Ah, yes. That would be Kerangani." Dewey nodded. There wasn't anyone in Hamilton who didn't know all about Cedric Hasting's two years as visiting priest in a tiny East African village. "That was quite a long time ago," she commented. "Twenty-five years, at least."

"Before my time," the young man responded easily, propping a knee on the dashboard. "Since Dad died, I thought it might be kind of—the thing to do, to stop in and see his old buddy. I was coming East, anyway—never been East."

"No?" asked Dewey with a smile. "Well, Hamilton isn't exactly the East—but I'm sure you'll find that out when you get to New York or somewhere. Where are you from?"

"California. Central Valley. So this is pretty foreign territory to me.'' He grinned disarmingly. ''I feel like I could get lost here. It's pretty countryside.''

'' 'Roaming like a dream the ever-silent spaces of the east'? It is pretty,'' agreed Dewey.

''What's that—poetry? Or is that how people talk in Hamilton?''

''Tennyson,'' said Dewey with a laugh. Her passenger looked too old to be still in college. A graduate student, perhaps, taking some time off from his studies. ''You're making a grand tour, then, I take it,'' she said in a leading tone.

''Yeah—taking it slow. Came up here on the bus from St. Louis this afternoon. Hope to make it to Washington in a week or so.''

''An old-fashioned cross-country tour.'' Dewey felt slightly envious. ''Well, I'm pleased that you found time to stop in this part of the world. Rather off the beaten track, isn't it?''

''I guess—but I don't like the beaten track much. And I figure that if I find a place that feels like home, I can just stay for a while.''

''An enviable frame of mind. And Cedric will certainly be glad to meet you. I'm surprised he didn't come to collect you at the bus depot.''

Harrison Powell laughed good-naturedly. ''Don't blame old Cedric. He doesn't know I'm coming. Thought it might be fun to surprise him.''

Dewey absorbed this information thoughtfully. ''Well, I am sure he will be delighted to see you anyway,'' she responded politely, with a glance at the well-stuffed knapsack. The young man probably needed a place to stay, if even just for one night. There wasn't another bus out of Hamilton until morning.

Dewey wondered what kind of a welcome he might get at the rectory. Cedric Hastings wouldn't think twice about asking him to stay; in the old days the good rector had been famous for taking in strays, who usually stayed a week or so, living in the attic and earning their keep by doing odd jobs around the church. One of Cedric's most famous strays had stayed for two years and supervised the installation of the new steeple at the church.

But Cedric Hastings wasn't the man he used to be. At sixty-three he was, of all things, a newlywed—or almost. Two years previously he had married, seemingly out of the blue, a tall, beautiful young woman called Charlotte French. Their union had surprised Hamiltonians—many of whom tut-tutted and responded with cagey remarks about men of a certain age; but to Dewey the marriage seemed solid. Heaven knew Cedric was happy enough, with the beautiful Charlotte to wash his socks and bear him a child.

"He's married, you know," she told her passenger. "With a baby."

"No! Really? Dad always thought Cedric was the world's happiest bachelor."

"And so he was. Now, however, you may count him among the world's happy husbands."

"Hah." Harrison Powell laughed softly. "A contradiction in terms." He turned and looked at the dog in the backseat. "Hey, fella," he remarked.

Isaiah gave him a tentative stare and then, making up his mind, uttered a low, soft growl.

"He doesn't approve of your views," Dewey remarked with a laugh as she made the turn onto High Street.

"Knee-jerk response. People expect it of unattached young men. No offense, big guy," said Powell, reaching back and scratching Isaiah behind the ear. Isaiah growled, and Harrison Powell withdrew his hand.

"In my day it was the young women who played hard-to-get," replied Dewey.

As the car slowed, Powell glanced up and down the street appreciatively, noting the trim, quaint beauty of the centuries-old frame houses. "Just the way I always pictured it. We don't have houses like this out in California," he remarked. "Not in my neighborhood, anyway."

"No," agreed Dewey amiably. "Nothing like this. Just three-hundred-year old stucco. Charming, I think—and so exotic."

"If you like Spanish."

The car slowed in front of Number Four, and the young man called Harrison Powell smiled and stuck out his hand. "Thanks a lot for the ride," he said warmly. "Hope I get to see you before I leave."

"Oh!" Dewey was suddenly—and for no good reason—sorry to think that Harrison Powell might leave. He was a most agreeable young man. They could use people like him in this little town. "Oh, yes. Yes, indeed," she replied enthusiastically. "I'm sure we'll meet again."

Dewey turned the car and headed back down High Street, watching with interest as the door of the rectory opened, and Harrison Powell stepped over the threshold.

2

"YOU'RE CERTAIN THAT you don't mind, my darling?" Cedric Hastings asked his wife. They were in the rather dilapidated kitchen of the old rectory; Cedric leaned up against the worn Formica counter, watching attentively as Charlotte stirred tomato sauce on the stove. Harrison Powell, having been invited to dinner, was amusing himself in the den with photographs of his parents and Cedric from their Kerangani days.

From a huge cage in a corner an aged and dirty-looking parrot began to deliver a long, moronic stream of chatter. Underfoot a black-and-white cat meowed pitiably, from force of habit. It knew full well its pleas would be ignored.

Charlotte French, unperturbed by the chaos in her kitchen, added pepper to the sauce.

"Why would I mind?" she asked at last, her voice soft and reasonable. "There's plenty of supper." Charlotte knew perfectly well what Cedric wanted; but she was going to wait for him to articulate his request before granting it. This was one of the little lessons she had learned in two years of married life.

"Do you know, I think perhaps he needs a place to stay, as well," Cedric said finally in his best off-the-cuff manner. His voice rang with sincere spontaneity. Forty years in the pulpit had been a good training ground for oratory and persuasion; Cedric excelled at making the most carefully plotted speech sound extemporaneous. He paused. "It strikes me that it would be the kind thing to do to ask him to stay. The proper thing."

If only he would just say that *he* would like it! thought

Charlotte impatiently. And not spend so much time rationalizing a perfectly normal impulse. She smiled at her husband and waited for him to continue.

"Seriously, Charlotte," Cedric went on. "You know I wouldn't just open our home up like a boardinghouse. But he is Dan and Lucy's boy, after all."

Charlotte laughed gently and planted a kiss on her husband's cheek. "As long as he doesn't stay forever." She gave her husband a searching look. "What is it about Dan and Lucy Powell?"

"What is it? Nothing at all. They were my friends."

"Uh-huh. When you feel like telling me about it—" She broke off as their young son, Ben, emitting a gleeful shriek, began to hurl sliced carrots from his high chair onto the floor. The parrot, thus goaded into speech, began to spew forth a stream of grating, unintelligible syllables. Charlotte still had trouble believing Cedric's claim that the bird was speaking in ancient Greek. To her, it sounded like gibberish. But then, it would—Charlotte was not a classicist, and the parrot knew only a few words.

"Quiet, Pindar," said Cedric. The bird was instantly silent, but the little boy continued to hoot with laughter.

"You, too, Ben." Cedric, stooping to pick up the fallen carrots, made a comically ferocious face at his son; Ben shrieked in delight, and the bird once more began to offer a running commentary. The cat meowed, and Cedric, after making sure Charlotte's back was turned, gave it a heartfelt though restrained kick.

Charlotte went back to the tomato sauce, ignoring the swirling cacophony. She dipped a spoon into the sauce and held it out toward Cedric. "Taste it for me?"

Cedric tasted. "Perfect." He reached over to the spice rack against the wall and took down the oregano. Charlotte smiled and left him to it. This was her husband, the Reverend Cedric Hastings, the king of tomato sauce. It was only natural—he had been a vegetarian for fifty years, and he had spent most of the evenings of his chaste bachelorhood in perfecting this, his one great meal.

Charlotte, on the other hand, was a carnivore. Giving up serving meat at home hadn't been difficult for her, but she occasionally still indulged in a hamburger when she went out with her old friends. Now she gave the tomato sauce a wistful stir, thinking longingly of sweet and hot Italian sausages.

"I'll tell him, then," said Cedric. With a precise, finicky gesture he screwed the top back on the oregano and put the jar carefully back in its place. Then he headed for the small den off the back hall to invite Harrison Powell to stay with them for a while.

Charlotte leaned over Ben's high chair and wiped her son's mouth and chin. "We have a guest, baby face," she said to him. "You'll be a good boy, now, won't you?"

Just a year old, Ben had attained that state of pure baby bliss when mealtime holds out unalloyed promise—the joy of a romp in the most delectably soft substances known to human-kind. Now he smiled and reached out a grubby hand, daubing his mother's cheek generously with applesauce.

Charlotte laughed and pulled him up out of his high chair, dancing him around the kitchen in her arms. "Oh, you," she said softly, nuzzling his little ear. She was content. If only Pindar the parrot would disappear, she reckoned her life would be perfect.

If anyone had suggested, three years before, that Charlotte French's life would take such a turn, Hamiltonians would have goggled in disbelief. As a single young woman possessed of beauty, breeding, and a fair fortune, Charlotte French had been famous for her caprices and her zest for fast living. She had once fleetingly considered a career as a race-car driver; and although she hadn't followed through, the impulse was typical of her. By the time she reached twenty-eight years of age, Charlotte had traveled the globe on her own; had made and lost an easy bundle in the stock market; had learned to skydive, to hung big game in the West, and to climb rocky cliffs. She had even spurned an offer of marriage from a handsome member of the English aristocracy, the son of a duke.

Perhaps it was some element of danger, invisible to all but herself, that had drawn Charlotte French to Cedric Hastings. He was thirty-five years her senior, a quiet scholar of the scriptures and of Latin and Greek, with little interest in the ways of the outside world. In its very simplicity, his mode of existence seemed exotic to Charlotte—as outlandish, in its way, as the tribal practices of native Papua New Guineans might seem to the sturdy everyday folk of Hamilton. Even more outlandish, really; for Charlotte had been to New Guinea and found the natives not at all surprising. Whereas Cedric, with his quiet ways, passionate faith, and simple pleasures, left her breathless with amusement and anticipation.

It was true that Charlotte had had to spend the first six months of their marriage throwing things away; she had disposed of an amazing quantity of old magazines, broken box springs, worn-out shoes, and other detritus of Cedric's single-minded bachelor existence. But Charlotte was cheerful, if firm; and Cedric had yielded happily to her superior skills of home economy and tidiness. On two scores only was he adamant: the bird Pindar (who conversed all day long in parrotty fragments of Greek) would stay; and the black-and-white cat Eddie (who was Charlotte's—a relict friend from her single days) was to go.

Charlotte, however, hated parrots fully as much as Cedric hated cats; and so a truce had been forged. In this uneasy union wrought by their owners, the two animals watched each other warily, day in and day out; Pindar hurled incomprehensible abuse at Eddie, who merely smiled his cat-smile and slunk to a spot under the radiator, where he dreamed up ways to torment the bird without being observed.

Cedric and Harrison Powell joined Charlotte in the kitchen.

"It's awfully nice of you to have me," said Powell, smiling warmly.

"No problem," replied Charlotte simply, wiping the applesauce from her cheek. "We're glad that you came and looked us up. Cedric is always talking about Kerangani."

Powell laughed. "Yeah, that's the kind of experience that people talk about all their lives. Dad sure did. He never got over it." Powell sighed again. "Can I help with something?"

"You can set the table," responded Charlotte with the straightforward simplicity that Cedric loved in her. "And after dinner you can do the dishes."

Over dinner Harrison Powell talked about his father. Dan Powell had been a live wire—a complicated blend of passions and faith. As a clergyman, he had been tremendously popular. His congregation found him by turns stimulating and reassuring; they enjoyed watching his monumental struggles with temptation, the rigors of which he recounted in his sermons.

Dan Powell loved parties and staying up late to argue with his friends about life and theology. The renegade son of a stern New England bishop, he had been in and out of minor scrapes throughout his youth; but age had tamed him somewhat, and at the watershed of thirty years he had finally followed his father's lead into the church.

In the ordinary course of things Dan Powell and Cedric Hastings would never have been friends. But two years in Kerangani, a remote little one-horse town in the highlands of East Africa, had brought them together. In that tiny community Cedric had shed some of his air of disapprobation, and Dan had grown briefly more solemn. And then, of course, there had been Lucy—Dan Powell's wife. She was sunny and warm, alive with joyous laughter that bubbled forth in a constant stream. Lucy Powell had meant a great deal to Cedric. She had teased him out of his stern moods, but kindly, in friendship. He could remember even now, twenty-five years later, how her high spirits could make him momentarily giddy.

On a forested African mountainside, with colobus monkeys swinging through the trees overhead, wood hoopoes calling, and the stealthy forest elephants watching warily from the safety of the undergrowth, Lucy Powell had laughed at Cedric. Greatly amused by his stubbornly monastic way of life, she had sat down in a small clearing and pulled a bottle of wine from her rucksack. With the sunshine catching her golden hair, she had explained, wide-eyed and in the most patient terms, that hair shirts had gone out of fashion. The memory of that day had stayed with Cedric Hastings long after other memories of Africa had faded. Lucy Powell had been dead now for many years.

He glanced across the table at Charlotte, who was responding politely as Harrison Powell talked of his life in California. Cedric wondered what Lucy Powell would have made of his wife; what she would have thought, had she been alive to see her son sitting here at Cedric's table, in this quiet little rectory in Hamilton. He studied the young man—his thick golden hair and blue eyes, so much like Lucy's; his ready laughter and great physical ease in the world. Harrison Powell had inherited nothing of his father's looks, but seemed to have all of Dan's high spirits and irreverence. The young man who sat across the table from him appeared to be a complicated amalgam, thought Cedric. And not, really, like either Dan or Lucy. But intriguing; most definitely intriguing.

3

"GEORGE! YOU DON'T mean it!" exclaimed Dewey James in amazement, impatiently brushing back a few strands of her silvery hair and eyeing her friend with suspicion. "Harrison Powell is staying in Hamilton?"

It had been just over three weeks since Dewey had given Harrison Powell a lift to the rectory. In that time the young man had become entrenched in Hamilton life—an enduring stray, she had thought to herself. Now, however, it appeared that he wished to stay on permanently. It was decidedly odd, thought Dewey.

She had encountered the young man several times in town. There was something rather fascinating to Dewey about the ease with which he had slipped in amongst them. But with each encounter Dewey grew slightly less enamored of him. The charm had begun to wear thin.

"Looks that way, my dear," responded Farnham, helping himself to a cracker. "He's buying Cedric's old family place, out on Palmer Road."

"You're joking, George," said Dewey sternly. George loved to pull Dewey's leg.

"It's true, my dear. I promise." George Farnham looked affectionately at his friend and raised his hand in the Boy Scout three-finger salute. "I have it on the Most Sacred Authority."

Dewey's curiosity was piqued. "Whose?"

"Julia Boucher's."

Dewey was amazed. There was no doubt that George

11

Farnham had his facts straight, if he had got them from Julia Boucher. She was Cedric Hastings's right hand—had been for forty years—and she knew everything about him.

Felix Hastings, Cedric's brother, had died a year ago, leaving the family estate—an ancient house and thirty-two acres of forested land on Palmer Road—in Cedric's sole possession. Everyone in town knew that Cedric had long been looking for a buyer for the old place; he planned to use the money to fund a new church home for the elderly.

For the longest time, however, there had been no success. Only one prospective buyer had emerged—Mackenzie Munitions, Inc., a manufacturer of shotguns and hunting rifles. The company proposed to use the place as an executive retreat. But to Cedric, the idea of hunting for sport was anathema—a fact that everyone in town knew; and so he had refused to sell to Mackenzie, even though the proceeds would have funded the Elder Care House. This much Dewey had learned from Doris Bock, proprietress of the Tidal Wave Beauty Salon.

To say that the house needed work would be a kindness; the big old frame structure had been standing empty for nearly a decade. It still boasted two glorious old chimneys, however, and the grounds were magnificent. Dewey supposed it might be an attractive purchase for a young man of means with time enough to fix it up.

Dewey pursued her train of thought aloud. "He only came for one night—and he's been here almost a month. Now you tell me he's buying Cedric's old family place. What *can* be wrong with him?"

"What makes you think anything is wrong with him, my dear? The Hastings place is rather nice."

"George, nobody wants that old place. Cedric has been trying to sell it for more than a year now! It's perfectly astonishing. Don't you think so?"

"Seems reasonable enough to me." Farnham leaned back comfortably in Dewey James's well-worn red armchair and reached out for his glass. His demeanor was that of an habitué—which indeed he was. He counted himself Dewey James's closest friend; and it must be owned that some of his neighbors suspected there might be more than simple friendship behind that devotion. It was well known that Dewey and

George dined frequently together—more frequently than mere friendship might require.

Outside, night was falling, and the gentle, rolling countryside was settling in to receive the chill of a mid-November frost; but here in the snug parlor of Dewey's cheery farmhouse, the air was warm and inviting.

George Farnham looked contentedly about him at the familiar disarray of the room. On an oak rolltop desk in the corner were stacks of magazines and library journals; Dewey, officially semiretired from her post as town librarian, kept herself up-to-date. Against the wall stood two tall, glass-fronted bookcases, their contents showing clear signs of frequent use. A rosewood table under the front window held a pair of small silver dishes, a glass bowl full of seashells, and a silver-framed photograph, now worn and crackled about the edges, of Dewey's late husband, Brendan; he was seen here looking handsome in a naval officer's uniform, gazing out over the gunwale of an immense battleship.

A bronze clock on the mantel ticked loudly; its rhythms punctuated the gentle snores of Isaiah, who was sound asleep at Dewey's feet. George noticed for the first time that Isaiah was beginning to show a little gray around his muzzle. Getting old, thought George Farnham.

"The market is slow, Dewey. It's a good time to buy, if the price is right, you know." George chuckled.

"On, yes—no doubt the price was good," Dewey pursued. "But I think he has some kind of—of, I don't know, George. An agenda. He's like the Man Who Came to Dinner," she finished rather lamely. She would have been hard pressed to explain herself; but suddenly she was filled with discomfort. There was something not quite right about the situation.

Harrison Powell had planted himself, like a tenacious weed, in the fertile soil of Hamilton. Or—not quite like a weed, thought Dewey. Like some kind of strange, beautiful flower that required constant pruning to keep it in check. Or an *Ampelopsis*, she thought, recalling an apt analogy from one of her favorite authors. "Third week—all over the shop," she mused aloud.

"I don't know what you're going on about," said George, rising to pour himself another glass of sherry. "He's made himself quite useful in town. Seems a nice enough young fellow. Aimless, that's all that's wrong with him. Do him good to have a project of his own.''

Dewey had to agree that Powell had proved himself valuable. He had a flair for administration and, as it emerged, a degree in finance. Dewey had learned that he had taken over much of the church's day-to-day financial business from Cedric, who had a passion for thrift but little patience for paperwork. Harrison Powell had helped Julia Boucher to organize the annual church charity auction; he babysat for little Ben Hastings; and he even ran errands for Charlotte. All in all, not a bad sort of houseguest to have. Dewey reflected, with a cynicism unusual for her, that Powell had made himself remarkably agreeable to all concerned. She wondered what on earth he was up to.

''George—don't you think it's odd, the way he just stayed?''

''Not at all. Good for the town, get some new blood in here.'' George was used to Dewey's flights of fancy. He found them charming, if often strangely accurate. He went on with his tale. ''Julia told me all about it. I went to see them about renewing the lease on the rectory.'' Farnham had given up most of his law practice a few years back, but he still performed small services for a few important clients. ''Powell and Cedric signed the contract this morning. He's evidently planning to make Hamilton his home, my dear.''

Dewey pulled a sweater closer about her and sat, deep in thought, for a moment. ''I don't know what to think, George. But you know, I have a feeling there is more going on here than meets the eye.''

''Come, now, Dewey,'' said George. ''I think you're imagining things. What on earth do you find wrong with the man?''

''He's too good looking,'' said Dewey mulishly. George laughed. ''Don't you snicker at me, George. You know perfectly well that I have a nose for these things.''

''Ah, yes, so you do. I recall that you said the same thing about Grace's latest beau.'' Grace was Dewey's daughter, who lived in San Diego.

''Yes,'' said Dewey with triumph in her voice, ''and I was exactly correct. You will recall that he turned out to have no money and two wives.''

''*Two?*'' George chuckled heartily. ''I only heard about the one. You said he was married.''

"I said that he had been married twice. I never mentioned a divorce," said Dewey and laughed in spite of herself. "Have you spoken to Cedric?"

"Only just popped in at the rectory on my way here. He gave no indication of how he feels—but then, he wouldn't. Well, you know Cedric. Always chipper."

"I do indeed know Cedric. Always chipper, and about as confiding as a goldfish. You never know how he really feels about things. He talks in such abstractions all the time. What about Charlotte?"

"Charlotte wasn't there. She was off at the toddler group with their little one—what's his name?"

"Ben."

"Come, my dear. Forget all about the good rector, and let me take you to dinner somewhere nice."

"Oh, no, thank you, George. I have too much to do here this evening." She gestured toward the pile of library journals. "With Tom Campbell away in the south of France, I'm back to running the library single-handed."

"Is that so?" asked George, gently. "Well, my dear—perhaps you should see about lining up a little help. I don't like to think of you working full-time for half pay."

Dewey smiled. George was a Scot, after all. "You know perfectly well that help is not in the library budget for this winter. Besides, Tom will be back in ten days."

"Spouting bad French, no doubt."

"No doubt," agreed Dewey with a chuckle. Tom Campbell was rather given to showing off.

"Too bad that Cedric refused to sell to Mackenzie, though," continued Farnham. "I heard that old Stewart Mackenzie made quite a sweet offer."

"You know Cedric couldn't do that, George. He doesn't believe in guns."

"Nobody was asking him to shoot anything, Dewey. It would have been just business." George looked at Dewey with mischief in his eye. "He ought to climb down from that high hill of his every now and then, mix with the groundlings."

"Oh, you know Cedric. He's in another world."

"You can say that again. Won't he be surprised if he winds up in our boat in the hereafter!" Farnham laughed at the thought.

"Be kind, now, George. He's a clergyman, after all, and supposed to be a little bit better than the rest of us."

"So he is, my dear. So he is—supposed to be. Do you think he is better?"

"Well—he certainly works at it, anyway," replied Dewey, with a laugh. "I wonder, now, what he's up to with that young man. It's fishy, you must admit."

George noted with alarm the mischievous, speculative look on Dewey's face. He knew how her curiosity was likely to carry her into strange waters. There was no need for her to speculate about this situation. George was convinced that there was nothing fishy about it.

"Dewey?"

"Oh, relax, George."

"My dear, if you will allow me to say so—it's really none of our business what our neighbors do."

"No?" Dewey's eyes twinkled. "But then, George, for what do we live, if not to make sport for our neighbors?"

Uh-oh, thought George. He arose, pulled a gray cashmere muffler about his throat, kissed Dewey fondly on the cheek, and took his leave.

4

In spite of the cold of the November night, the small music room upstairs at the Church of the Good Shepherd was enormously hot. As usual, the ventilating system was out of order; and as usual, Wally Penberry, director of the Hamilton Music Society, took no notice.

In the back row of the alto section, Cecilia Parker pulled off her sweater and tried to make herself comfortable on the velvet-cushioned pew, reflecting bleakly that Wally took the notion of warming up just a little too far.

Cecilia looked up over her music and studied, with a mixture of puzzlement and pride, their newest acquisition: Harrison Powell. Cecilia had been surprised when he turned up at rehearsal; although, like everyone else in town, she knew exactly who he was: Cedric's latest orphan—the perfect Adonis of the rectory attic, and the new wonderment of Hamilton. He had been in residence a full month.

Cecilia almost giggled aloud at the thought of it. Poor Charlotte! Well, she had married Cedric, so she must have known of his habit of taking in wanderers. ''All we like sheep,'' she hummed to herself. Come to think of it, perhaps Charlotte herself was just one more sheep for the fold. Cecilia blushed at such an ungenerous thought and looked once more at Harrison Powell, who was studying his music with grave attention.

Wally Penberry called for attention, and Cecilia looked at him fondly, taking in the animation on his large, open face, the half-moons of perspiration that showed under his arms, the unfashionable flare of his trouser legs, and the endearing absurdity of his mismatched socks and old black sandals. Every inch a musician, Cecilia thought, with not a moment's fear of looking ridiculous. His obliviousness lent him dignity, even a certain superiority. How nice it would be to rise in the morning without a care about what one put on! Her own outfit had been carefully composed—a handknit sweater in Icelandic wool, a form-fitting red turtleneck; a pleated black tweed skirt (perhaps just a half-inch too short, she admitted), new stockings, expensive shoes. Well—a woman on her own again after two decades of marriage had to look her best.

The room seemed more crowded than ever tonight. The altos, who were always crushed in at the far side of the room, found themselves forced into an unceremonious commingling with the basses. Cecilia Parker looked around for the cause of the cramped quarters. She spotted it and nudged the dark-haired young woman to her right.

"Wally's harp," said Cecilia.

Ruth Speas looked around in annoyance. "I know. Wasn't he supposed to unload that thing at the auction?"

"Who would buy it?" Cecilia asked good-naturedly and laughed. "It looks like we're stuck with it for another year."

"Oh, Lord," replied Ruth. "I suppose we'll be doing the Britten for Christmas, just to get some use out of it."

"'Wolcum yole,'" replied Cecilia. An enormous affair encased in a huge black case, the harp was a great source of amusement to choir members; Wally, who was an organist of international repute, had snatched up the antique monster at an auction several years before; and every October he tried to sell it in the Good Shepherd's annual auction. It hadn't sold; it would probably never sell; and it brooded over them tonight, poised uncertainly on an upturned crate, looking like an enormous vulture, or a coffin for a giant.

"It doesn't look quite safe there. Looks like it might just fall right over and hit somebody."

"Got any ideas?" Ruth Speas nodded across the room at a tall, good-looking man of fifty or so, with wire-rimmed glasses, unruly gray hair, and the attitude of a movie star trying to ignore a crowd of moonstruck fans. He ran a hand casually through his hair and looked with unseeing eyes at the women across the room.

"I know what you mean," agreed Cecilia Parker. She had little liking for Owen Bennet, the tenor soloist. He had a magnificent, rich voice, but an ego as big as all outdoors. In the course of his career with the Music Society, Bennet had broken the heart of every soprano in the room; nor had he restricted his romance to the choir. He had quite a reputation in Hamilton as one who liked to play fast and loose with married women.

Not for the first time Cecilia was glad that she sang alto. Owen Bennet had no use for altos; and as a consequence, she had never had to go to the mat with him.

"Top of page forty-four, please, everyone," said Penberry. "Quartet, are you ready? 'Libera me,' in four. On the downbeat."

"One moment, Wally," said an earnest silver-haired soprano. This was Mirabelle Meissen, a precise and disapproving Swiss woman. "Please to tell them that they are not to sing 'Jay-zoo,' but 'Yea-soo.'" Mirabelle Meissen shook her head mightily and scowled at the other singers.

"Yes, thank you, Mirabelle," replied Penberry, with a good-natured smile. "'Yea-soo,' choir." In the back row of the alto section, Elsie Resnick, the soloist, made a face and rolled her eyes. Mirabelle was too much.

"Her day wouldn't be complete without that," whispered Elsie.

"It's a wonder we do anything right, being mere ill-educated Americans," agreed Judy Stebbins.

Penberry plunged ahead with the music. He leaned into the piano, and the voices of the choir swelled, struggling against the complications of the fugue, sorting themselves out, rising, crescendoing, then finally reaching the reassurance of the final chord, like a wave relaxing, at last, on the beach.

The rehearsal proceeded smoothly, as well it might. The Hamilton Music Society was well practiced; most of the singers had been members for a decade or more. Some of them sang on Sundays, at church; the others—less spiritually inclined, perhaps, or of different faiths—belonged just for the fun of singing in the thrice-yearly concerts, which were always well received in town.

The group boasted four professionals, most of them students

or teachers at the Weaver Institute of Music in nearby Leesburg. This quartet took the solo parts and were paid—if not handsomely, then at least respectably—for their efforts. But otherwise the group was entirely amateur and utterly enthusiastic.

Since joining the Music Society, Harrison Powell had been infected with the same lively enthusiasm; and he had been welcomed with open arms, for he sang beautifully. Last week Owen Bennet had missed the Sunday service, and Powell had stepped in. Word was that Wally was thinking of asking Powell to become a permanent soloist, trading off with Bennet. Cecilia wondered how Bennet—who took his musical reputation in deadly earnest—would react to such a blasphemous suggestion. Cecilia hated to generalize—but you just never knew, with a tenor. And Owen Bennet was well known for his temper.

As the choir reached the end of the last movement, Wally Penberry nodded, glanced at his watch, and smiled broadly.

"Good. Wonderful. Think you can remember all that on Sunday?"

"Sure," put in Arthur Garrison, the bass-baritone soloist. "Just stoke us up with Julia's punch." He was a strongly built man in his early forties, with the air of a mountain man lately returned from chopping wood.

"Amen to that," agreed Elsie Resnick. Julia Boucher's punch was well known in Hamilton as the most potent brew this side of moonshine. The choir parties were always the most astonishingly festive affairs.

"Ah, yes." Penberry raised his eyebrows and smiled impishly, his large moon of a face alight with pleasure. "Not to worry, Arthur. Now. Let's run through the whole piece from start to finish. Ready? On the downbeat."

Before she headed out into the cold air of the evening, Julia Boucher stopped in for a quiet look about the darkened church. She always did so on Wednesday nights, after first making sure that the Music Society rehearsal got off to a good start. Julia Boucher did double duty on Wednesdays—first putting in a full day at the church office, where she worked as Cedric's secretary, and then tending to the needs of the choir, providing tea and cookies. On concert days she made sure the robes were clean and brought her famous punch to the party.

There was something magnificent and reassuring about this church in the dark; the massive repose of the dark oak pews, the looming silence of the walls, the tentative light shining through three stories of stained-glass windows. Julia liked to be alone in this darkness, with the lusty voices of the choir reaching her faintly from the music room upstairs, and the peace of the evening within her.

She could hear the scraping of chairs and laughter as the choir broke off its singing momentarily. How she wished she had a voice! It always seemed like such fun—that ill-assorted group upstairs, brought together by one simple talent. True, some of them were really remarkably good—Elsie Resnick had a majestic, rich alto voice, and Maggie Merrit, the leading soprano, sang like an angel. Julia seated herself quietly in a pew and listened, wondering briefly what would become of Owen Bennet. She had overheard Wally's conversation with him today (as indeed Julia overheard most of what went on in the offices of the church); and Bennet had been distressed. That was putting it mildly, actually; he had been incensed, loudly and understandably angry. Furious, even—he had threatened to quit the Music Society altogether and had finally stormed off, mumbling something about lawsuits. Well, that was Owen Bennet. When he wasn't suing someone, he was breaking hearts.

Julia roused herself and carefully placed a small cashmere beret on her head. She was getting on in years, but everyone agreed that she was remarkably fit for seventy-two. Even Cedric Hastings agreed; he had promised to put her in charge of admissions to his Elder Care House when he got the money from the sale of the house.

The Elder Care House provided a timely opportunity for Julia. The diocese had been suggesting, ever so politely, that it might be time for her to retire from the Good Shepherd; their suggestions, she knew, would soon become a request. But she could have her job with Cedric, and there might even be a housing stipend included with it, if they played their cards right.

Thank heaven Cedric had finally found a buyer for the old wreck! Although Julia had urged him to swallow his principles and take the offer from Mackenzie Munitions. Julia was devoted to Cedric, but she thought his views on hunting strange, and she always had. Julia had been a fair shot, in her day. Well, those were the old days.

She hoped she would be up to the job. Lately, she had discovered in herself a desire to drop off to sleep in the most inappropriate places. If she wasn't careful, she'd wind up snoring in the pew all night. She pulled her woolen coat about her and stood.

Up in the gallery the wind sighed heavily, and there was a creak, followed by a soft susurration, as though someone had reached out gingerly to touch the organ, then swiftly changed his mind. Julia made a mental note to ask Wally about the new bellows, due to be installed next week, thanks to the money that the church auction had raised this year.

Perhaps, thought Julia, as she picked her way through the dark toward the side door, she would ask Wally around to supper, by way of celebrating the bellows. Maybe she would ask that nice young man to come by, as well; Harrison Powell had single-handedly been responsible for half the money raised by the auction. Heaven knew what he had found to buy, among all the old rugs and broken-down bicycles and used china for sale; but Cedric's old house certainly could use furniture. How odd, that he had decided to stay in Hamilton, and buy Cedric's old house. But it had worked out nicely for all concerned.

In the cold air of the church parking lot, Julia Boucher pulled her coat and scarf closer about her. She was surprised to see a solitary figure across the way, under the shadow of a big old locust tree. A man was standing quietly with his hands in his pockets, looking out over the small graveyard next to the church. It looked like Cedric Hastings. What on earth was he doing out here in the cold?

"Cedric?" she called.

The figure turned. Cedric Hastings was a slim man, tall, with wire-rimmed spectacles and a sallow complexion that was at odds, somehow, with his curly steel-gray hair. Tonight he wore a long, free-flowing black cape and a wide-brimmed black hat, making him look, to Julia, like something out of the Salem witch trials. He stepped into a small pool of light cast by a streetlamp and looked at her without speaking.

"Cold night for old bones, Cedric," Julia said with a laugh. "What are you up to? Making sure they stay put?"

Cedric removed the hat and bowed stiffly from the waist.

"Good evening to you, Julia." His voice was lilting, almost musical, and his diction was perfect. The effects of forty years in the pulpit, it must be owned; but pleasing nonetheless. "I trust you got the choir practice off to a good start this evening?" He walked softly toward her.

"Oh, yes. The Mozart *Requiem,* you know."

"Always a popular piece. Good. Julia—remind me tomorrow that we really ought to raise the ticket price."

"I already thought of that. What do you think of four dollars?"

Cedric whistled. "Steep—but the Music Society is worth it, wouldn't you say?"

"For the Mozart, absolutely. We have to pay all those orchestra members from the Weaver Institute."

"Ah, yes, so we do," Cedric replied unhappily. "I don't suppose there's a way around that little expense?"

Julia laughed. She and Cedric had a similar conversation every year before the Fall Concert. The orchestra was expensive; that was true. But what else could you do? You couldn't perform without musicians. Besides—Julia knew the truth. Half of the audience who filled the church for their concerts came to hear the orchestra. Sometimes she suspected that the other half of the audience was composed entirely of the choir's family members, dragged by their ears.

"You know Wally always charges what the traffic will bear." Julia looked around. Cedric's old Volkswagen was nowhere in sight. "Can I give you a lift home, Cedric?"

"No, thank you. I'm going to wait for Harrison Powell; we need to discuss one or two things. And I want to step into the church office for a moment. Good evening." He donned his hat and strode briskly away into the darkened church porch. Julia could just make out his shadow as she put her car in gear and headed home.

"Et lux perpetua," sang Julia Boucher softly to herself, as she negotiated the turn onto Howard Street. "Luceat eis."

5

THE WIND CHARGED down from the north, an icy wedge that ripped with the efficiency of a machete through the little river valley. The early November sun shone with fortitude but with little effect; the day promised bitter cold. On the streets of Hamilton people bustled about in unaccustomed layers of wool, darting hurriedly into the warmth of houses and automobiles, eager in their efforts to dodge the freezing blasts that reddened their cheeks and made their eyes water.

The careful observer, well bundled against the wind, might have had time to note a hint of extra excitement in the air. For this was the day of the big Fall Concert at the Church of the Good Shepherd. Although the Hamilton Music Society gave three concerts a year, it was always the November performance that drew the most interest and the largest crowd. As a prelude to the riotous holiday season that would shortly and inevitably follow, the Fall Concert stood out as a true harbinger of winter festivities. What *The Nutcracker* is to Radio City, the Fall Concert is to Hamilton.

Small wonder, then, that Josie's Place—the cozy café that was the heart of Hamilton at lunchtime—was jammed with a festive group. Although she did not usually keep her establishment open on Sundays, Josie herself was there this day, presiding cheerfully over steaming bowls of oyster stew, mushroom-and-barley soup, and toasty sandwiches on French bread—her unvarying special menu for concert day. Her cash register rang and her waitresses scurried in an atmosphere of lively anticipation. But at three-thirty sharp Josie's Place would be utterly still; Josie was quite a fan of the Music Society. She was looking forward to the Mozart *Requiem;* it was one of her favorites.

In a worn oak booth with a soft leather seat (the very same spot where Samuel Clemens is said to have once lunched), Dewey James and George Farnham were settled in comfortably. Last year, for Dewey's birthday, George had treated her to season tickets to the Music Society; and Dewey felt it would be small of her not to invite him. Even if that had been his intention all along. And really, if she put her mind to it, she didn't know anyone who would enjoy it more than George—in spite of the lure of televised football. He really was rather touchingly devoted to her.

Josie approached their booth. She was a tall woman, with dark curls and deep-set green eyes that had seen a great deal, one way and another, over the years. Hamilton kept few secrets from Josie.

She smiled at George and Dewey, who were well known to her. "Well, well, you two. Up to your neck in scandal, as usual?"

Josie rarely mingled with her patrons; she preferred to supervise her well-trained staff from her habitual perch on a creaky old swiveling stool near the cash register. From this coign of vantage she had a clear view of all the proceedings within her establishment.

"Hello there, Josie," said George with a twinkle. "To what do we owe the honor of such estimable personal service?"

Josie placed two steaming bowls of soup before them, put down her tray, and accepted George's offer of a seat.

"Cold day for the concert," she remarked with a sideways look at Dewey. "Have you heard?"

Aha! thought Dewey. Josie must have interesting news. Josie often had interesting news.

George was eager to hear. "Out with it, my friend." He smiled and tasted his soup. Josie was uncommonly skilled at concocting sublime but simple dishes; George, widely regarded as possessing the most sophisticated palate in town, lunched here most days.

"Well," said Josie, "the concert is going to be just a bit different this year."

"Ah, yes?" asked George with relish. He loved departures from tradition, no matter how small or inconsequential. He shook pepper on his soup. "Tell."

Josie nodded cautiously toward the counter, where Cecilia Parker was taking a solitary bowl of oyster stew. "From the horse's mouth, you know." She leaned in. "Owen Bennet is not singing."

"What?" Dewey was really shocked. Owen Bennet had been the tenor soloist in the Hamilton Music Society for more than two decades. "You're joking! Is the concert canceled?"

Josie shook her head. "No way. Not old Wally. They've asked the Wonder Boy to step in."

"Heavens!" Dewey was thrilled. A real scandal! There was no question whom Josie meant by "the Wonder Boy"— Harrison Powell. Well, well. Dewey had been waiting for this. She knew that, one way or another, the beautiful young stranger had been destined to stir up their little town.

Josie went on to explain. The rumors, which had been buffeting Hamilton's music lovers for a full three days now, were true—Harrison Powell had replaced Owen Bennet as the soloist in the tenor section. "Cecilia Parker told me that Owen and Wally had it out in the orchestra rehearsal yesterday. And Wally dismissed him. *Right* in front of everyone. Owen was under the weather again." She shook her head.

Dewey and George understood the euphemism. Owen Bennet had a drinking problem; this much was common knowledge. But in the past he had always managed to work around it.

"Do you suppose Harrison Powell is up to it?" asked Dewey, worried that the concert would be spoiled.

"I'm sure he is, my dear," put in George. "Wally wouldn't let us down."

"I suppose not." Dewey looked at Josie. "Poor Owen," she said, with a sympathy that was perhaps more wished for than felt. Owen Bennet was difficult, even on his good days. And those, in recent years, had grown fewer and fewer. "He must be terribly distressed."

The situation seemed to amuse George, who had little fondness for the displaced drunken tenor. "Oh, pish-tosh. He'll get over it. And he'll be back, getting on Wally's good side, appealing to Julia and Cedric. You watch—he'll sing the *Messiah*."

"But, George, that's not the same, and you know it." Dewey shook her head. "The *Messiah* is only tradition. A convention. Whereas the Mozart is a concert."

"She's right, you know, George." Josie stood. "I have to get back to things. See you both there." She smiled and departed, leaving Dewey and George to digest her story.

"Oh, dear, George. You know how Owen takes on. Wally knows perfectly well what Owen is like. He probably would have been just fine today. What do you think got into Wally?"

"Don't know what got into Wally. But I know what got into Owen Bennet. The demon rum."

"Poor Cedric will hear about this, no doubt. *And* poor Julia Boucher." Dewey knew well that Julia, Cedric's right hand, was often called upon to run interference at the church office. "You know how Owen gets when his nose is out of joint."

"His nose is never *in* joint," George pointed out, with absolute accuracy. "That's probably why he hits the bottle all the time."

"You don't like him, George, but I feel rather sorry for him. He has been singing all the big parts for twenty years."

"All the more reason for him not to get soused before a rehearsal. Anyway, it's time to give someone new a chance. It's not as though it were Carnegie Hall, Dewey."

Dewey thought about this. Her friends in the big cities assumed that life in the Hamilton countryside—with its quiet hillsides, genteel horse farms, stands of ancient forest, and swift-running river—was merely picturesque. Dewey supposed that her New York acquaintances might have sniffed at this afternoon's concert and made light of Owen Bennet's tragedy. But there it was, on the landscape of their life; and in Hamilton this tragedy was large and important.

"I suppose you're right," she agreed at last. "Perhaps it will blow over."

They began to talk of other things—there was never a shortage of interesting topics for such keen students of the human condition. George Farnham, as president of the town council and a semiretired lawyer, had his ear to all the town's political doings, such as they were. And Dewey, from her post at the circulation desk in the small but excellent library at the center of town, saw and heard a great deal.

Hamilton, for all its quaint charm, was no stranger to

violence, intrigue—even scandal. People were people wherever you went, Dewey liked to point out. Her late husband, Brendan James, had been the captain of the town's little police force for many years. Since his death Dewey had had more than one occasion to drop in at headquarters—for Brendan's successor, Fielding Booker, was an earnest but sadly plodding detective. In recent years Dewey had discreetly assisted Bookie (as the good captain was known to his friends) in solving one or two unfortunate crimes in the otherwise peaceful little town.

"At any rate," George was saying, "I hear that Powell is very well settled out at the old Hastings place. I ran into Michael Kayon today."

"The architect."

"That's the one. Harrison Powell was talking of hiring him to refurbish the house, starting from the ground up."

"Good heavens! *That* will be a job."

"You're telling me," agreed George. "Says Powell wants the whole thing reconstituted."

"Like orange juice."

"Mmm. Anyway, Kayon went out and had a look around. Said there is a lot to be done, but he thinks the whole shebang could easily be completed by spring. Meantime, Powell is getting ready to set up camp for himself in the downstairs area—the kitchen, with a little room off it for his bedroom."

"Remarkable." Dewey shook her head. She did not understand Harrison Powell's fixation—for it was a fixation, she was sure—with the old Hastings place. But she let it pass—it was time for them to make their way to the concert.

A cheerful audience was assembling in the old church. In spite of the increase in ticket prices and the biting cold, there was a very good turnout—very good indeed. Dewey was momentarily surprised; but she quickly realized that everyone else, by now, would have heard the story of Owen Bennet's dismissal. There was nothing like a little neighborly curiosity to fill the house, she reflected. And Harrison Powell was a drawing card—there could be no doubt.

Dewey and George seated themselves comfortably in the high gallery that lined the upper walls of the church. There was a silver lining to every local scandal—the place was completely filled. She settled in and looked around, spotting many of her

friends and neighbors in the audience. In the front pew, with a
rakish felt beret firmly in place, sat Julia Boucher, ready to
appreciate every note. Next to her, upright and attentive, was
Cedric Hastings. There was no sign of Charlotte; perhaps she
hadn't been able to find a sitter for Ben.

Dewey thought Julia Boucher rather remarkable. For forty
years she had been Cedric's right hand, never wavering in her
devotion to the Church of the Good Shepherd. Even when
Cedric took his post in Africa, Julia had kept the place running.
Without Julia, Dewey wondered how Cedric would manage.
She studied them, the picture of solid friendship. Was this how
she and George looked to their friends and neighbors?

Dewey wondered, not for the first time, how Julia felt about
Cedric's marriage. Certainly Charlotte's presence at the rectory
had altered their relationship; Dewey could recall a time when
Cedric and Julia had been inseparable. She had made him
dinners and fussed over his personal life, helping him when it
was time to hang new curtains in the rectory, accompanying
him to dinner parties and the theater. All of that, of course, had
changed when Cedric fell for Charlotte French. But the town
rumor mills had been silent on the score of Julia and Cedric; no
word of any kind of falling out had reached Dewey's attentive
ears.

The orchestra took up their instruments. The choir filed in,
looking if not resplendent, then at least colorful in their
well-worn purple robes. Finally Wally Penberry, neatly groomed
and glowing with pride, bowed and took up his baton. They
were off.

The sweet strains of the music so pleased Dewey that she
was slow to notice the disturbance that had begun several seats
away. As the quartet took up the third movement, the "Tuba
mirum," Dewey shifted uneasily and looked to her left, where
Owen Bennet was leaning heavily over the balcony rail,
waving his program furiously. Just as Harrison Powell came in
with the tenor line, Bennet let out an obscene shout of laughter.

"You call that a voice?" he cried drunkenly. "Ho! The
Wonder Boy!"

The audience began to murmur; in the pews below, people
turned their heads and looked at him, scowling and embarrassed. Dewey could see the rage that began to burn a slow
course across the face of Mirabelle Meissen. George Farnham

leapt to his feet, pushed hastily through the row of people, and made his way to Bennet's seat.

The choir and the orchestra struggled on mightily while George put a heavy hand on Owen Bennet's shoulder. He talked softly to the tenor, who responded with another sloppy peal of laughter. Finally George Farnham managed to lead Bennet out of his seat and down the back stairs. The audience and the musicians recovered themselves, but Dewey spotted Cedric Hastings in one of the pews below. She noticed with dismay the look on Cedric's face. She thought she had never seen anyone look so angry.

As the concert ended, the audience made its slow way out. In spite of Bennet's pitiable lapse of manners, the performance had been well received, and Dewey, as she headed out to the front steps to look for George—who had never returned to his seat—heard the approbation in the comments of her neighbors.

"Well, well," said George, locating her in the crowd and taking her firmly by the elbow. He spoke softly. "Let's go, Dewey, before they buttonhole us for details."

Indeed, George had a point. Dewey noted the approach of Doris Bock, proprietress of the local beauty parlor and purveyor, *par excellence,* of local gossip. Dewey and George scurried down the stairs, and he hustled her into his waiting car.

Up in the music room a subdued Hamilton Music Society changed out of its robes and into its street clothes. The women, discreetly cloistered in a small room at the back of the parish hall, shook their heads and muttered to each other. Mirabelle Meissen, naturally, had quite a lot to say on the subject of unruly American tenors; but her comments were steadily ignored by altos and sopranos alike. Maggie Merrit, who had indeed given a glorious performance, looked shocked and tired. Elsie Resnick managed a philosophical shrug of the shoulders. She had been singing with Owen Bennet for twenty years; and while she prized his voice and his great stage presence, she tended to agree with Wally that he had outlived his usefulness to their small group. It was too bad, but there it was.

Before very long, however, the group began to recover its usual bonhomie. After all, they still had the party to look forward to, downstairs in the common room.

By the time the singers had joined the orchestra members for the party, the shock and solemnity had been replaced with an air of levity. Indeed, under the influence of Julia Boucher's famous punch, the incident seemed rather to enliven the party; even Wally Penberry, who had earlier seemed distressed, began to feel better. Before ten minutes had elapsed, Penberry was seated happily in a leather sofa, telling anecdotes about the great composers and congratulating his choir for the teamwork and musicianship that had pulled them through the great crisis.

"What do you do with a drunken tenor?" sang Steve Krall, the bass baritone. Arthur Garrison took up the song, jumping up on a chair, punch ladle in hand, to conduct. Soon everyone had joined in, even those who might have felt a twinge of pity for Owen Bennet. Only Harrison Powell seemed to resist the merriment. He was leaning up against a wall, next to a large flower arrangement, looking awkward and sadly out of his depth.

Elsie Resnick joined him. "This room always reminds me of funerals," she said. "This is where people come to greet the family, afterward."

"It's a pretty room," said Powell, looking about at the carved oak panels on the walls, the handsome furniture, and the large urns of flowers.

"I guess so," Elsie shrugged. "Maybe I've just lived in this town too long. I've been to a lot of funerals." She looked closely at Powell, her dark brown eyes shining kindly. "Don't take it to heart," she said finally. "Owen gets that way. It's his problem, you know—not yours."

Harrison Powell smiled a sad but handsome smile and ran his long fingers through his golden-blond hair. "I keep thinking that if I hadn't turned up, and been so eager, none of this would have happened."

Elsie looked at him steadily. "You could be right," she agreed in a mildly speculative tone; she was not one to brush aside uncomfortable truths, nor to be led to emotional extremes by someone else's display of temperament. "On the other hand, you're not responsible for his behavior at the rehearsal yesterday. After the dustup with Wally he tried to pick a fight with the first violin."

"No kidding."

Elsie nodded matter of factly. "No kidding. I heard it from

the bassoon. All in all, you know, I think we're very glad you turned up.''

"That's kind of you.'' He glanced across the room at Maggie Merrit, who still looked stricken. "Maggie doesn't look very happy. Too bad—she sang so beautifully today.''

Elsie followed his glance. The soprano soloist did indeed look distressed. "She probably left her smelling salts at home,'' said Elsie in an amused whisper. "She's an Artiste— sensitive, you know.''

"Ah,'' said Powell. "A star's constitution.'' He smiled at his companion appreciatively. "You're an artist, Elsie. How come you don't have fits?''

"I'm an alto. We're different.'' She laughed her musical contralto laugh and took Powell by the arm. "Come on and have some punch.''

The party began to pick up. Wally Penberry, now perched atop a large oak table, surveyed his little group with delight. They really had pulled through for him—especially Harrison Powell, who had managed to learn the music for the tenor part in short order. Powell's voice, it was true, needed training; but he had a natural talent that was a great boon to them all. He watched in pleasure as Powell sidled up to the punch bowl and held out his cup to Julia. That young man would fit in well, Penberry reflected. He wouldn't pick fights with all of his fellow musicians.

It had been an exciting day, and a tiring one; it was now late, and before long the singers and musicians began to think uncomfortably of the burdens that awaited them in the work week ahead. Soon Julia's punch was gone, and soon, too, were most of the revelers. Arthur Garrison and Steve Krall were among the last to leave. They headed sturdily out through the parish hall, arm in arm, reprising their song about the drunken tenor. Wally Penberry planted a warm kiss on Julia's cheek and thanked her for the party.

"You sure you don't need my help cleaning up?'' He glanced about the room, now littered with paper cups and plates.

"I'll stay,'' said Harrison Powell.

"We'll both stay,'' volunteered Elsie Resnick.

"Get on with you, both of you,'' scolded Julia. "You leave

that to me. You young folks have got things to do. Go on, now.''

Wally and Elsie, knowing that they wouldn't win this one, departed; and Powell, after one last attempt to persuade Julia to accept his help, put on his hat and coat and headed out through the darkened church. Julia was alone in the familiar little room.

All in all, the day had been a success. But Julia wasn't certain she liked the new tenor so well. At least with Owen Bennet you knew where you stood; but this young man struck her as being a little too eager. "Eddie Haskell," she said to herself. "Wanted to help me clean up. Just like Eddie Haskell."

She began to mutter quietly to herself as she picked up the detritus of the revels. It wasn't a big job; the choir members, mindful of her age, were always remarkably good about tidying up as they went along. When the last paper cup had been dispensed with, and the famous punch bowl washed and cleaned and put away for next time, Julia headed back through the darkened church and up the stairs to the music room. She wanted to be certain that all the music and the robes had been put away properly.

Forty years of working at the Good Shepherd—as Cedric's secretary and unofficial party-giver to the choir—had given Julia Boucher an uncommon familiarity with the building. She was not afraid of the little noises that came with the night; she felt not a moment's hesitation as she swiftly headed for the darkened stairwell behind the church and began her slow, steady climb to the top.

Once she reached the top landing, she groped instinctively for the switch that powered the lights in the music room. She flipped up the small metal tongue; nothing happened. But Julia Boucher, ever practical, kept a flashlight in the small music storeroom—which was really no more than a closet at the back of the music room. She plunged ahead through the darkness, bumping her bad knee on one of the chairs.

"Ouch!"

There was a small, answering rustle from the back of the room.

Mice again, thought Julia, making a mental note to borrow Elsie Resnick's cat for a few days. Last winter the mice had made their nest in a box that contained fifty copies of a

Vaughan Williams mass; Julia wasn't certain they'd ever be able to afford to replace the copies that had been ruined.

She put out her right hand and felt her way along, keeping close to the wall to avoid running into Wally's piano bench. In the darkness she could feel, rather than see, the huge shape of the harp case, poised in its little recess, looking blacker than its surroundings. It loomed over her as she made her way slowly and carefully along the wall. She heard again the rustling noise, but by now her mind was on the flashlight. She was rather proud of that flashlight, was Julia; Cedric and Wally had both scoffed at her foresightedness. But now they would see how clever she had been! She knew just where it was—in the little cabinet to the right of the door in the music storeroom. She walked past the rack that held the purple choir robes, hanging silent and still now like mute sentinels, like Bluebeard's wives. Julia felt a chill.

She found the flashlight and went about the business of sorting through the music, making sure that all the scores had been returned, and straightening the items in the storeroom. She gave the dial of the safe—which held the receipts from today's concert—a vigorous twist. Then, clutching the flashlight carefully to her, she departed.

As she left, she was assailed by an unfamiliar nervousness. Had she been alone in the darkened offices of the church? There had been such a noise—too much for just mice. She had felt as though someone watched her in the darkness. Very likely it was her imagination, getting ahead of her.

6

CHARLOTTE HASTINGS WAS not, in the ordinary course of things, a woman who took other people too much to heart. Make no mistake—she was generous and kind and in her thirty years had developed close friendships with people of both sexes and all ages. But she carried within herself, at the core of her being, a self-sufficiency that amounted, on occasions, to sang-froid.

It was this self-sufficiency that allowed her to take enormous risks; to have learned, for example, how to jump from an airplane at five thousand feet, and how to travel around the world on her own. This same self-sufficiency created within her a fixed set of boundaries; Charlotte knew who she was, and where she was going, at all times. And while she loved her friends very much, and sympathized with them tenderly, she nonetheless did not always keenly share in their emotional highs and lows.

Thus it was that Charlotte had been, for the month since Harrison Powell's arrival, unable to understand the emotional restlessness that had overtaken her husband. She sensed that there was something that had been unresolved in her husband's relationship with Dan Powell, Harrison's father; but Charlotte was a woman who liked to get on with life. She knew perfectly well that Cedric Hastings hadn't seen the Powells since their departure from Kerangani twenty-five years before. She was at a loss, therefore, to comprehend the morass of nostalgia that had overtaken Cedric.

That is—Charlotte supposed it was nostalgia. For the four

weeks that Harrison Powell had been a guest in their house, Cedric had seemed to grow more and more distracted. There was little doubt that the parishioners noticed the change as well; just last Sunday Elsie Resnick had stopped by the rectory for tea after the service. It was unlike Elsie to take such a step, for her real interest in the church, as everyone knew, centered around Wally Penberry's music programs. Cedric had once said that Elsie would sing for Lucifer himself, provided the old man asked for the right song. Elsie probably would have agreed with this assessment.

On the Monday following the concert, Charlotte bundled little Ben into his stroller and headed for the church. She often stopped in to lend a hand at the office, because poor Julia Boucher was sadly overworked. And even Harrison Powell, who had begun to do odd jobs for the parish and to put in time balancing the accounts at the end of each week, couldn't take up all the slack. With any luck the church would have a new computer by next spring, which would make the business end of things run more smoothly. Unless, of course, using the computer proved to be more work than doing things the old-fashioned way. But Charlotte Hastings was a forward-looking woman, and she had great faith in the tools of the modern age.

It was a bright, cool morning, with puffy clouds overhead and a hint of warmth in the sunshine that filtered down through the old locust trees that lined the street. The church was less than half a mile away, on the other side of a small park, and Charlotte took pleasure in pushing her small son along the quiet pathways that led to the Good Shepherd parish house.

Attending to church business was still a fresh challenge to Charlotte. She continued to be surprised by her own level of interest in parish matters; in the past, all of her activities had been flashes in the pan, gripping her fiercely for a month or two, being supplanted, quickly, by the next hot trend or the next exciting travel destination. But Cedric's church was her church now, too. She had come to enjoy the role of minister's wife, serving tea at the vestry meetings and opening her dining room once a month to the members of the parish council.

She was sorry to have missed the concert yesterday; and sorry, too, that she had not been present for the great Incident. Cedric had returned home rather late, still full of wrath at Owen

Bennet's behavior, and had spent the remainder of the evening apologizing to Harrison Powell. To a point, Charlotte had thought, that went far beyond what the occasion required.

Thinking about last night brought Charlotte once again to her preoccupation with Cedric. He was out of sorts; there could be no question about it. Every attempt to question him had been met with a polite but firm rebuff.

There was between her husband and Harrison Powell something that unnerved her. She tried to took at the situation objectively; and she had to admit the possibility that she was jealous. Since Harrison Powell's arrival, Charlotte had begun to sense that there was much about her husband that she would never know. Before they married, he had lived an entire lifetime, almost; she had been little more than an infant when Cedric and Dan Powell had forged those intense bonds of friendship in Kerangani.

Still—that sense of being left out couldn't explain Charlotte's relief at hearing that Harrison intended to move to the old family house. There, too, something was strange. She considered it odd that anyone would think of living in that old house; but she was grateful that Powell had bought it. Thanks to the money from the sale, Cedric's Elder Care House would soon be a reality.

Charlotte was so immersed in her thoughts that she passed right by the church door and continued down Howard Street to the center of town. When she finally realized where she was, she had arrived at the door to Josie's Place.

"Oh, Ben," she said to the infant, who was gurgling cheerfully in his stroller. "Maybe a little snack would set Mommy straight. What do you think, baby?"

Ben seemed to agree that this was a good plan; he waved his hands and let out a little squeak of laughter, and Charlotte pushed open the door of the café.

The place was quiet; there weren't usually many customers before lunchtime, although Josie was thoughtful about being open for business bright and early. Hamilton was a country town, and the local horse breeders and farmers liked to drop by for a doughnut or a quick chat with their neighbors after seeing to their feed orders or calling at the bank.

Charlotte looked about. Dewey James was seated at the counter, enjoying a leisurely cup of tea; Charlotte remembered that the library always opened late on Monday mornings. And off in the farthest booth was Doris Bock, proprietress of the Tidal Wave Beauty Salon.

Oh, no, thought Charlotte as she smiled at Doris. She'll be running off now to tell her customers that I wasn't at the church office this morning. Sometimes it could be confining, the life of the rector's wife in a small town. She ignored the obvious invitation on Doris's face, settled herself into a booth, and ordered a cup of coffee.

She was stirring in the cream, lost in thought and staring at Ben, when she heard a familiar voice.

"Devoting the morning to the secular side of life, eh?"

Charlotte looked up. It was Harrison Powell, that persistent ghost. Couldn't she even escape for a cup of coffee without being haunted by his presence? Charlotte blushed, embarrassed by her unkind thoughts, and gestured to the seat opposite. She forced herself to be polite.

"Ben and I are playing hooky. Don't tell Cedric."

Powell ordered a cup of coffee and returned his attention to Charlotte, smiling warmly at her. "Rely on my discretion. But—won't it be obvious? I'm sure Cedric is there by now." He glanced at his watch, and Charlotte felt suddenly resentful that this man should know her husband's schedule so well. But this morning he was wrong.

"No. He didn't go into the office this morning. He's gone to call on old Mrs. Hatfield. She's got the flu."

"That the butcher's wife?"

Charlotte nodded. "Cedric doesn't proselytize, Harrison. You know that. He doesn't expect his whole flock to become vegetarians." After two years of marriage to Cedric she had learned to forestall this kind of question; it was almost a reflex, although she realized that she didn't need to spell it out for this man. He seemed to know Cedric almost better than she did these days.

"I know," agreed Powell. He injected his voice with his customary heartiness, which had begun to grate on Charlotte's nerves. Nobody could be as cheerful as Harrison Powell. It was just too much; she suspected that, deep down, he didn't really care for her much. "Well," he began again. "I've been to talk to Michael Kayon about the old homestead. He thinks

I'll be able to move in, set up a kind of camp for myself, within a week or two.''

''Really?'' Charlotte was surprised. The last time she had seen Cedric's old family place, it had looked like a haunted house to her.

Powell nodded. ''The kitchen and the little room off the back of it are perfectly adequate for me now. I went out there with the building inspectors this morning, and the old stove is working like a charm. Plumbing, too, in that little section. So I think I'll be moving in this week some time. Have myself a little adventure in the country. Going to buy kerosene lanterns and a goose-down sleeping bag and do some thinking.''

''Sounds like a monastic retreat,'' said Charlotte.

''Look, Charlotte,'' said Powell awkwardly. ''I want to say thank you for everything you've done for me. This has been a difficult time of my life, after losing Dad last year. I know that it was Cedric's idea to have me stay.''

''Oh—'' Charlotte broke off and waved it away. She wasn't accustomed to offering soothing platitudes—and she did feel that her hospitality had worn thin. Powell put out a hand and took one of hers in his own.

''You've been a good, kind friend to me. I want you to know that I appreciate it.''

''Don't worry about it, Harrison.''

He took a quick sip of coffee, looked at his watch again, and rose. ''I'm late. I promised Julia I would help her with the utility bills this morning.''

Charlotte Hastings was suddenly overcome by remorse for her lack of generosity toward this strangely troubled young man. She smiled. ''Ben will miss you when you go, you know.'' She glanced at the boy, now sleeping soundly.

''Not as much as I'll miss him.'' He leaned down and chucked the baby under the chin. ''See you for lunch?''

Charlotte nodded and watched him go, oblivious to the eager curiosity in the watchful eyes of Doris Bock.

From her seat at the counter Dewey James, too, had watched the little scene with great interest. Being a more sophisticated observer of human nature than Doris Bock, Dewey leapt to a different kind of conclusion.

There was a time when she had known Charlotte fairly well;

Dewey remembered her as a vivacious and entertaining school-girl, popping up twice a week at the library in search of the latest thriller; or taking out *Harriet the Spy* for the fifth time in a month. Dewey, like the rest of Hamilton, had been thoroughly surprised by Charlotte's marriage to Cedric. Bright but a bit wild was how Dewey had always thought of her.

Charlotte Hastings looked anything but wild this morning. In fact, thought Dewey, gathering up her belongings, Charlotte looked rather distressed. She was sitting stock still, almost indifferent to the sleeping little boy in the stroller, staring after the man who had just departed.

"Good morning, Charlotte," said Dewey, pausing in her progress to the door. Dewey hated to intrude on the young woman's solitude, but it would be rude to pass by the table without at least saying hello. "That young man gave quite a performance yesterday, you know."

Charlotte smiled. "So I hear. I heard about the rest of the performance, too."

Dewey shook her head. "Poor Owen Bennet. That was really most unfortunate. I always think it's much better not to make a show in public, if you can help it."

Charlotte laughed—the first good laugh she'd had in ages. Everyone in town knew that there was no one who was better at taking a public stand than Dewey James—when she felt the circumstances warranted extreme action. She was idiosyncratic in the extreme and little afraid of public censure when she had the forces of Right on her side.

"Won't you sit down, Mrs. James?"

"Oh—I really should go along to the library."

"Please. Ben would enjoy your company." Charlotte smiled down at her son, who had awakened and now stared with cheerful eyes at Dewey. "He looks just like my father when he sleeps."

"Does he, now?" replied Dewey, intrigued by the remark. "Well, just for a moment. Thank you." Dewey sat and looked carefully at Charlotte. "I know it's really none of my business," she began, "but you look tired, child."

"I'm sure I do. The strains of young motherhood."

"And the strain of a four-week houseguest on top of it, no doubt."

"Oh, dear," said Charlotte with a humorous sigh. "I hope it doesn't show."

"Good heavens, girl, you'd have to be made of iron to withstand that kind of assault on your home and hearth."

"He's really most helpful. And his father, you know, was one of Cedric's great friends."

"Yes—so I have been told. He is the talk of the town, my dear."

"Hardly surprising," said Charlotte, feeling her good spirits beginning to return. She had always liked Mrs. James. "We don't get many handsome young strangers wandering into town and settling in for good."

"You know, I did hear something that surprised me. Is it true that he's bought the old Hastings estate?"

"It is. Kind of amazing. Cedric is pretty thrilled about it—he thought he would never find a buyer for the old place. And the money will come in handy for the new Elder Care House."

"I'm sure it will." Dewey regarded Charlotte with interest. "It bothers you, doesn't it? That young man moving into Cedric's family place."

Charlotte took a deep breath. "Somebody had to buy it, Mrs. James. And I think it's nice it could be one of our friends."

"Well, dear," said Dewey with a smile, "I'm sure that things will settle down nicely, once everything is settled. When is moving day?"

"This week." In spite of herself Charlotte grinned broadly.

"That's wonderful." Dewey rose and leaned down to take a closer look at Ben. "Everything will soon be back to normal."

She took her leave of the young mother and headed off to the library, where ranks of books awaited her tender care.

7

IN THE CHURCH office on that same Monday morning, Julia Boucher was shaking her head. Her thin, sharp-featured face showed the strain of the last two days. She had not begun to recover from the distressing Incident at the concert—when Owen Bennet had come so close to turning the big day into a fiasco. Nor could she forget the eerie feeling that had possessed her last night when she had gone to put the scores away in the music room. And now, as she carefully counted up the ticket stubs and tallied the money in the cashbox, she was having trouble concentrating. Either that or the totals did not match. But that was impossible. Who would believe that someone in Hamilton would take money from the church's receipts? But as Julia worked her way through the figures for a third time, she again came up short. They seemed to be missing more than three hundred dollars.

She looked up at the large round black-and-white clock on the far wall. Nearly ten-fifteen, and she was still the only one here. Where was Charlotte? Tending the baby, of course; but the baby was usually quite happy in the church office. And what about that young man? What had Cedric told her? He was going off with the building inspectors to look at the old homestead, that was it. Ridiculous, his buying that place.

The whole thing was very odd, thought Julia. She had liked Harrison Powell at first; and certainly she had welcomed his expert advice on various questions of finance, for he seemed to know a great deal about business. But there was something odd

42

in the way he had attached himself to their little community. Julia Boucher had devoted her life to the church, and to its fine and intelligent rector, Cedric Hastings. She did not welcome interlopers.

"Good morning, Julia." Cedric had arrived, his cheerful voice and perfect diction slicing like a knife through the membrane of her reverie.

Julia looked up with a start. "Hello, Cedric. How's Mrs. Hatfield?"

"She'll do. Needed to have her hand held a bit, that's all. What are you daydreaming about? All that money? It's a grave responsibility." Cedric hung his coat on the old bentwood rack in the corner of the office, then approached the front desk where Julia worked. He gazed down at the little pile of cash. "But hardly enough to bankroll a trip to Acapulco."

"Cedric, we're three hundred and six dollars short." Julia looked at him, her eyes worried.

"Aha!" Cedric's tone was buoyant. "A thief in our midst. Who do you think it can be?" He pulled up a chair and turned Julia's notepad toward him, comparing the ticket stubs with the cash receipts and checking over her multiplication quickly. Multiplication had never been Julia's strong point.

"Hmm. I declare you're right." A streak of worry crossed Cedric's brow, but he banished it. "Who can it be?" he asked with a smile. "Was it you?"

"Oh, Cedric, don't."

"Not you. I believe you. And I can promise you that *I* didn't take it—word of honor. Charlotte was at home with the baby, and that only leaves the ladies of the parish council who took in the money at the door. The Hammond sisters, if I'm not mistaken."

"You know perfectly well it wasn't Alice *or* Octavia."

"No, I suppose not." Cedric appeared to find the situation amusing. He often took things too lightly—always had, reflected Julia. He had a strange ability to deflect the irritations and problems of day-to-day life—a trait that often annoyed Julia deeply. But she knew from experience that it would do little good to argue. If she accused him of not taking the situation seriously, he would counter with a small sermon on the necessary burdens of temporal existence and their comparative insignificance in the universe. Julia wondered, from time to time, if Cedric had a heart.

"I think we should report it," she said stubbornly.

"Do you? I suppose you may be right. On the other hand, if anyone is so villainous as to steal from our penurious coffers, he or she may well be in desperate need. Don't you think?"

"Not as desperate as our need. We have to pay the musicians."

"There is that. However—perhaps we can strike a bargain with them. I tell you what, my dear. Why don't we just keep this under our hats for the nonce?"

"But, Cedric—it's so much money!" Julia was scandalized. What on earth was the matter with Cedric? Ordinarily, he would have been up in arms. He was fiercely jealous of the church's small income.

"I'm only being practical," he replied in a tone of annoying complacency. "After all, there isn't much one can do, really, short of frisking everyone who was there, or making poor Fielding Booker go from house to house arresting anyone who has three hundred and six dollars." He smiled at his old friend. "Don't worry. It's just a small amount—and there's always the world to come, you know, where such matters are more easily attended to."

Julia gave in, but she was not pleased. "All right," she said. She gathered up the money and locked it away in the little safe under her desk.

"Now." Cedric spoke smartly. "How about those letters we need to send to the diocese?"

"What about the letters to the state welfare office, Cedric?"

"Hmm?"

"About the Elder Care House."

"They'll have to wait. We must first placate the tyrants at headquarters with our reports." He pointed a finger straight up in the air. "Onward and upward, Julia. Let's get them." He goose-stepped comically into his private office—a large, well-lighted room, with handsome bookcases, an Oriental rug, and a comfortable leather sofa in whose luxuriant depths worried parishioners were wont to unburden themselves.

As the afternoon wore on, Dewey James was having a difficult time keeping her mind on her work. She looked about her in discouragement, wishing that Tom Campbell—the capable, if pompous, young man who had taken her place as head librarian—would hurry back from the south of France. Dewey hated to admit it to herself, but she wasn't up to this kind of full-time work anymore.

Two years before, when she had finally decided to retire, the time had seemed to hang heavy on her hands. Mondays were always slow at the Hamilton Public Library. And now that she was semiretired, Dewey was accustomed to more leisure—to more free time to follow up on certain ideas that occurred to her. Dewey always had ideas that needed following up; she was having one right now and wished that she could close up her beloved library and do a little thinking. There was something on her mind. She was worried about Charlotte Hastings.

The front door opened, and Dewey looked up to see her good friend Susan Miles—a pretty blond woman of about forty—arrive. In tow were two little girls.

"Hiya, Dewey," called Susan. Meg, who was five, and Elizabeth, eight, scurried to the circulation desk, chattering excitedly. They were great pals of Dewey's.

"Hello, you two ragamuffins," said Dewey, leaning over the counter to take a good long look at them. Elizabeth, the older girl, smiled shyly and seemed to debate shaking hands. Finally she stuck out her hand bravely, and Dewey shook, with great solemnity.

Meg watched this sober transaction and then looked at Dewey with wide eyes. "You have muffins for us?" she chirped in delight.

"No, my dear, no muffins. However, if you are a very good girl, I will show you a book that I've been saving just for you."

"A *book?*" Meg was disappointed.

"A very good book."

"With pictures of muffins?"

"No. With pictures of elephants."

"See, Meg," said Elizabeth with the confidence of one in the know, "I told you." She looked at Dewey. "I told Meg you would show us some books, Mrs. James.

"I will certainly do that. Do you have anything special, Elizabeth, that you might like to read?" Elizabeth was in the second grade and so far had demonstrated herself a fair critic of the literary offerings that came her way. Dewey liked to hear Elizabeth's opinions; she felt the girl gave good advice.

Elizabeth curled her left foot behind her right ankle and

raised a finger to her lips in contemplation. "Our teacher told us about the Pilgrims today."

"Ah, yes. Thanksgiving will be here soon," nodded Dewey. "Did you like the story?"

"No. I thought it sounded made up. I want to read something real."

"Aha," said Dewey, who secretly agreed that the party line on the Pilgrims was a little too sweet to swallow. "Well, then, how about a story about a horse?"

"Yeah!"

"Yeah!" added Meg, tired of being left out. "A big horse. And *no* elephants." Meg had opinions, too.

"All right, you two. Follow me." Dewey led them to the children's corner, a brightly colored area with plenty of comfortable cushions and bean-bag chairs. On a table against the wall there was an enormous supply of paper, crayons, and colored markers, kept on hand in case the desire to read should momentarily desert the library's young patrons. Dewey took down several selections from a bookshelf as Susan settled the girls in on their cushions; then the two women returned to the front desk for a chat.

"I heard about the great scandal yesterday," Susan remarked as she settled herself on a tall stool. Dewey took up her post behind the desk and began to sort through a pile of index cards. "According to Nick, George saved the day." Nick Miles was Susan's husband.

"I didn't see Nick at the concert," replied Dewey.

"Oh, no, he was watching football with the boys down at the Seven Locks Tavern. But after the concert everyone there heard all about it. You can imagine."

"Yes, I can." Dewey conjured up the image of the well-fed men's men of Hamilton, listening to the tale of the distraught tenor as they sipped at their beers at the Seven Locks. "Well, it was just too bad. I feel sorry for Owen Bennet." Dewey shook her head sadly. "He's a very talented man, you know. But he does have a problem, I'm afraid."

"That's what Nick said. We both think he ought to get some help."

"One would think so. But it's so difficult to help people."

"Anyway," pursued Susan Miles, "what I want to know from you, Dewey, is all about the Wonder Boy."

"Ah," said Dewey.

"Well, I think it's pretty strange that he turned up in town in the first place. Good name for him, the Wonder Boy. Because I wonder about him. Don't you, Dewey?"

"His father was Cedric's great friend, you know," said Dewey mildly. She felt no sudden urge to defend Harrison Powell, but she did think her own uneasiness about him was a little ridiculous.

"Right. But I think he's an opportunist."

"In what way?" Dewey was puzzled. Something in Susan's assessment struck a chord; but it was difficult to say exactly why.

"Well—Nick heard that there was another offer for Cedric's old place. A *better* offer. But he got all sentimental and sold it to his friend's boy. That's not right."

"Oh. Well, there was another offer. But Cedric didn't want to sell."

"Why not?"

"It was Mackenzie Munitions—you know, the shotgun makers from Leesburg. Being such a strict vegetarian, Cedric felt it wouldn't be right to sell them his family place to use as a hunting lodge. At *least*," said Dewey, pausing to consider, "I assume that was the reason." The two women looked at each other. "Well," said Dewey, "you know how Cedric is. Absolutely unshakable."

Susan laughed. "That's for sure. I can't get over how he's tamed Charlotte French."

"It *is* amazing," Dewey agreed.

They were distracted from musing on this extraordinary marriage by a frantic scream from the children's corner.

"Mommy!" Meg, her face contorted with terror, was making a beeline for the circulation desk. "Mommy! They took General Barker!" She waved a book desperately before her mother. "Look!"

Susan Miles rolled her eyes at Dewey. "I knew we'd be in for this some day."

The general thus referred to was not a military man, but the Miles's former dog, a crazy mongrel who had had little use for his family. Last month he had bitten the mailman for the third and final time; Susan and Nick, after much discussion and many sleepless nights, had finally resolved to send him away.

They had found him a job as a patrol dog at an old cemetery in the next town, which was a kinder alternative than they had hoped for. Now, however, they lived in daily fear that he would turn up again at their door, snarling and ungrateful, but home. The effort to replace the dog in Meg's affections with a small gray rabbit had thus far been unsuccessful.

"Let me see, honey," said Susan, taking the book from Meg. The book told the story of a dog who had saved his family from a flood; Meg was too young to read it by herself, but there were several large paintings of the canine hero of the tale. The dog delineated there, in all his seedy glory, did indeed bear a strong resemblance to General Barker. Dewey, reflecting on the undistinguished nature of the General's family tree, felt that half the mutts in the county probably looked just like him. But she kept her thoughts to herself.

Elizabeth joined the scene, her face full of an acutely grown-up concern. She looked at Dewey. "I think it scared her," she said. "Meg's still pretty little, sometimes."

Susan hoisted the sobbing Meg up onto her knee and looked at the drawings carefully. She stroked the little girl's hair gently as she turned over the pictures, and then she nodded. "Don't be afraid, sweetie. It does looks like General Barker, doesn't it? Maybe it's his cousin. Look—remember how the General had a little brown spot on the tip of his ear? This dog is different, see?" She pointed to the solid black ear tip in question.

Meg, however, had reached that pitch of emotion when nothing would do but a nap. She refused to be comforted; Susan, with an air of beleaguered amusement, gathered up her brood and departed.

Dewey, watching them go, considered what Susan had said. There was something wrong about Harrison Powell, the Wonder Boy—even Susan, who was deeply practical, had felt it. Dewey kept thinking that somehow he was too good to be true—like the seedy mongrel in the story that had frightened little Meg. No dog that looked so much like the infamous General Barker could really be a good dog, Dewey was convinced. General Barker had been bad through and through.

Dewey reflected on this train of thought some more as she reshelved books and tidied up. And when closing time finally came, she bundled herself into her coat and set off to call on George Farnham.

8

HARRISON POWELL, UNAWARE that his idyll as the Wonder Boy of Hamilton was about to end, betook himself on Monday evening to the Seven Locks Tavern, down where the canals meet the old railway junctions, alongside the river.

In its heyday Hamilton had been a very busy town indeed. Situated near the confluence of two large rivers—important freight routes—and a busy railway junction, Hamilton had been a nexus between agriculture and industry, a pretty little town that had flourished in an aggressive commercial age.

But that had been a century ago. Today Hamilton was not flourishing; it was only surviving, but it survived rather well. There was a good deal of wealth in the area, chiefly in the form of horseflesh; several established breeders of thoroughbreds found Hamilton most congenial to their enterprise. The town's civic life was up-to-date, in a small-scale, twentieth-century kind of way; there was a video store and a health club—both downtown on Howard Street, for the wise people of Hamilton had strenuously resisted the brutal indignity of a new shopping mall.

There were certain places in town where this pride in the past was even more keenly expressed. In one or two working-class neighborhoods—Canalside being one of them—the grandeur and the bustle of the nineteenth century still made themselves felt.

In the unprepossessing building that had once housed the splendid canal works, Nils Reichart had opened the Seven

49

Locks Tavern. Even today the place had an aura of tattered glory, and in the back room, if you were curious and looked carefully in the half-light, you would find leftovers from the great days of the canals. Over against a wall was an old heelpost; next to it, behind the pool table, was one of the enormous winches that had controlled one of the sluice gates; and doing duty as tabletops were massive sections cut from the old wooden caissons.

When Harrison Powell entered the Seven Locks on Monday evening, he was given a warm welcome. Although Nils Reichart and his patrons had eschewed yesterday's choral outing in favor of professional football, an account of the Incident had quickly reached the place. Owen Bennet was a very good customer at the Seven Locks, but he wasn't a favorite there—not by a long shot. He drank too much and was inclined to fight.

Powell pulled up a barstool and sat. Nils Reichart greeted him warmly and drew him a large schooner of ale. Reichart— who was, for a barkeep, a singularly cultivated man—would probably have preferred yesterday's Mozart to football; but it might not be good for business to admit it.

"Cheers, Reichart," said Powell, raising his glass.

"I hear you did a fine job yesterday," Reichart responded in a low voice. "We heard all about what happened." He nodded toward a booth in the farthest corner. From his barstool Powell could just see over the top of the booth; Owen Bennet was there, by himself.

Powell smiled easily. "Got to give the guy the benefit of the doubt."

"No, we don't," said Reichart, who was an old-fashioned man with strong feelings about the proper way to behave toward one's neighbors. "Got to give the guy a piece of my mind. That's what I should do." He shook his head and wiped the top of the bar with a greasy rag. "Anyway, I hope you won't take it wrong. The rest of the town seems to like you plenty."

"Sure hope so," said Powell with a faraway look in his eye.

"So your dad and old Cedric were pals out in the jungle somewhere—that right?"

"Yup."

"Long time ago. I was just a kid when Cedric Hastings went

off on his famous trip to Afrique. You weren't even born yet."

"Nope."

"It's good you came here. But I can't figure out, if you don't mind my saying so, why you stick around."

"Oh—well, I don't know myself, really. Just seem to find this a good spot. Lots of opportunities, built-in friends, like that."

Unnoticed by the two men, Owen Bennet had approached the bar. Now he grabbed Powell by the shoulder and spun him around. Bennet's face was white with rage and contempt.

"I know what you're up to," he said in a quiet, menacing voice. "And I'm telling you plain: Don't try your little games with us, pal. Lay off. If you know what's good for you. Understand?"

Bennet's voice, even at this pitch of emotion, was remarkably expressive. He looked steadily at Powell, who seemed not to notice the plain hatred in the older man's gaze. Or, if he noticed it, he counted it as nothing. Reichart, in spite of himself, was taken aback.

Harrison Powell suddenly looked very young, yet seemingly unruffled by the threat. For the first time since Reichart had heard of Owen Bennet's scene at the church, he wondered if perhaps it hadn't been justified. There was something unsettling in the dismissive confidence of the younger man. Harrison Powell had the look of someone who always got his own way.

"Come on, Owen," said Powell, his voice hearty but utterly without feeling. "Let me buy you a drink. No hard feelings, okay?"

"Hah!" Owen Bennet was disdainful. His fine blue eyes mocked Powell's coolness, and he turned to Reichart. "I'll have another. Put it on my tab, Nils." He glowered at Powell, then downed the whiskey in one swallow.

"Another." He pounded the glass down on the bar.

"Come on, now, Owen—" Reichart began.

"Owen, don't you think maybe you've had enough?" Powell laid an arm on Bennet's shoulder. Bennet, without warning, swung a mighty fist that landed squarely on Powell's jaw. He drew back as the younger man reeled, and got off another blow, this one to the solar plexus. Powell, doubled over in pain and fury, looked helplessly at Reichart as a small crowd began to gather.

Within seconds Reichart had pinned Bennet in a half nelson. He propelled him toward the door and shoved him unceremoniously into the parking lot.

Bennet stumbled and fell. As Reichart closed the door of the tavern, he was momentarily unsettled by the look on Bennet's face. There was something frightening about it.

"Sorry about that," the barkeep apologized. "Have another beer, Powell?"

Harrison Powell came out of his distracted study. "Thanks, Nils, I will." He smiled ruefully at the other drinkers. "Beer all around." He lifted his glass in a toast. "To my new friends—here's to us, and those like us."

"Damn few," put in one old man.

"And them dead," chimed in another.

They drank.

Dewey James had never intended to start anything by her inquiries about Harrison Powell, but in the days and weeks that followed, she bore a heavy burden of responsibility. By the end, of course, she knew her actions to have been justified. Even if she had never acted, the truth would eventually have come out; but she couldn't help thinking that, left to their own machinations, the players in the little drama might have rung down the curtain on a more benign denouement.

It started innocently. After leaving the library that Monday night, Dewey stopped by to see George Farnham in his house by the river. She wanted his opinion on the rumor that Susan Miles had heard—that Harrison Powell had somehow pulled the wool over Cedric's eyes in the matter of the sale of the house.

George had been a widower for several years; and after his wife's death he had moved from his family's comfortable farmhouse, not far from Dewey's house out on Hillside, to an old mill building in town. When George took possession of the mill, it had been a shell—a disused industrial space, unlived in and uncared for; but to escape the grief that gripped him, George had transformed it. He restored all the natural stonework and laid down wide-plank antique floorboards in every room. He put in a magnificent kitchen with sleek professional appliances, and an enormous sliding-glass door that gave out on the river. It was here that George's friends liked to come and sit and visit with him. That Monday evening Dewey seated herself at George's spacious oak table and filled him in on Susan Miles's visit to the library.

"Well? What do you make of it, George?" she asked her old friend, a touch of impatience in her voice. George was cooking; and when he cooked, he only had half a mind for the conversation. The Escoffier of Hamilton, he especially enjoyed making dinner for Dewey, whom he quietly adored. When he played his cards right, George managed to make supper for Dewey twice a week.

Dewey, if pressed, would have admitted that the arrangement suited her beautifully; her culinary skills, it was widely acknowledged, were not the best. On her own in her kitchen, with none but the dog Isaiah as a witness, Dewey stirred up an alarming and unorthodox succession of concoctions, which suited her just fine.

But tonight she had more important things on her mind than supper. She wished, sometimes, that George would pay closer attention to what was going on. She had the feeling, this evening, that he might listen politely and then just as politely dismiss her fears. She wanted him to go and be a lawyer and find out about a few things for her.

"What do I make of what, my dear?" asked George, stirring something. His abstracted tone confirmed her fears.

"Come *on,* George. Do you think that old Stewart Mackenzie was serious about buying the place?"

"Maybe, maybe not. Probably. He's a cagey old guy, but not one to make an offer if he doesn't plan to back it up." He grated some fresh ginger and stirred it into a large pan of vegetables. "But even if he were, Cedric probably would prefer things this way."

Cedric's dietary preferences and his pacifist notions had been constantly assailed throughout his long and virtuous life. He had withstood the pleadings of his parents, the jeering of his college classmates, and the temptations of adulthood, all without faltering. In this matter, at least, Cedric Hastings was not one to change his mind. As a teenager, Cedric had discovered Gandhi; and Cedric, who did nothing by halves, had thoroughly embraced the man's teachings. His commitment to pacifism had never been seriously tested—he was 4-F, thanks to a bum knee; and life in the gently rolling Hamilton countryside didn't offer much in the way of armed struggle. On the other hand, he had never been known, since the age of thirteen, to consume animal flesh of any kind. Cedric was rather proud of his record.

"You know how he is," George went on. "He may even think he's done that young man a service. Though I'm darned if I see what anybody wants with a run-down old place like that."

"A run-down old place on thirty-two acres."

George whistled. "Didn't realize it was that much. You know, Dewey, the taxes alone will probably break him—even if he does have deep pockets."

"Will he put up condominiums, do you think? Oh, George! Those awful people from Aviance Realty!" Dewey shuddered as she remembered a close call the town had recently had with a particularly unpleasant group of real-estate speculators.

"Don't see why he can't do just what he likes out there. It's his, you must remember."

"Yes, so it is. But somehow I don't trust him, George." Isaiah, reflected Dewey, had disliked Harrison Powell from the first. She recalled the day that she gave the handsome young stranger a lift to the rectory. Isaiah had growled at him from the backseat, resenting his air of familiarity and his free and breezy remarks. It wouldn't do to tell George about this, however; he would laugh at her, or be quietly polite. So Dewey kept her counsel; but she trusted Isaiah's instincts, and in this matter she felt the dog was absolutely right. There was something off about that young man.

"Don't you, now?" George arrived at the table bearing a steaming platter of sautéed shrimp and vegetables and a large bowl of rice. "Here you go, my dear."

Dewey looked with interest at the food. "What have you cooked up?"

George smiled proudly. "*La cucina orientala.*"

"Is that meant to be Italian, George?" asked Dewey with a laugh.

George gave her a wide-eyed look, took off his apron, and sat down. "Italian? Great Scott, no. Chinese, ain't it? Have some wine."

And so they dined, and no more was said that evening about the sale of the Hastings place.

The next morning, however, things began to happen.

* * *

The telephone at the library rang at nine-thirty.

"Dewey, will you lunch with me on Saturday?" asked George, without preamble. "I have a rather interesting proposition."

"A proposition, George?" replied Dewey, sounding distracted. She was typing up an angry letter to a publisher that had cashed her check without sending her the books she had ordered. "George, can I send you a copy of a letter? As a lawyer, you know."

"Of course, my dear. Listen to this." He was impatient. "I've been invited to go hunting."

"Hunting! George, you haven't been hunting in years. What is it—a snipe hunt with your college friends?"

George chuckled. "Nope, nothing like that. A real hunting trip—or a day of it, anyway."

"Who invited you, George?"

"Sit down. Are you sitting down?"

"Of course, George."

"The Wonder Boy."

"What?" Dewey laughed aloud. Harrison Powell was really taking Hamilton by storm. First the church, then the choir. Now he was clearly bucking for membership in the Marshy Point Ducking Club. "He's relentless, that young man."

"Certainly is. You know that the club allows nonmembers to have parties occasionally. Well, he's organized a dove shoot for Saturday morning, to be followed up with a picnic on the porch at the old clubhouse."

"George—I don't mean to sound snide—but why on earth did he invite you?"

"I'm a pillar of the community, my dear. In case you had forgotten." George sounded miffed.

"A useful pillar," said Dewey with a laugh. "He must want something from you. How did he arrange all of this, if he's not even a member at Marshy Point?"

"He's become buddy-buddy with Bruce Ward."

"Oh, yes. The senior guide. Well—are you going?"

"Oiling my gun as we speak, my dear. I have just time to get down to the post office for my dove stamp."

"Your what?"

"Permit. Dewey—listen. I thought it would be great fun if you'd meet me there for lunch. How about it?"

"Certainly, George. I will look forward to it. Shall I bring something for the picnic?"

Farnham thought hastily. Dewey's kitchen wizardry left much to be desired. "How about a nice Beaujolais?"

"Done."

"Bring two bottles."

"Two? George—"

"I hear the Wonder Boy had invited half the choir. And—believe it or not—he asked Cedric and Charlotte."

Dewey gasped. "You're joking, of course."

Many Hamiltonians felt some enthusiasm for hunting—after all, this *was* the country. People did still oil their ancient twelve-gauge shotguns and bag a duck or two—sociably, and in season. Mercifully for the ducks, the season was comparatively brief. Such sport held little appeal for Dewey. She didn't enjoy spending a freezing, wet winter's morning trying to hide from view among the reeds in a dank and icy marsh, waiting for some unsuspecting duck to fly fatally close. But she reasoned that if she didn't balk at the supermarket meat counter, she had no right to complain about shopping the old-fashioned way.

Cedric, however, was different, and there wasn't a soul in town who didn't know it. It was impossible that Harrison Powell, who had been Cedric's guest at the rectory for upward of a month, didn't know the clergyman's feelings on the subject.

"He declined, of course," remarked Dewey.

"They both did. Charlotte used to be quite a shot, you know, in her wild young old days. But she's given all that up."

"Yes, I suppose she has. I think she even sold her shotgun at the church auction this year. Honestly, that boy is either blind or heartless."

"Oh, I don't know, Dewey. I think perhaps, in the excitement of organizing the party, he simply forgot."

"Cedric must be fit to be tied."

"How would you ever know?"

Dewey laughed. Cedric Hastings was often impossible to read.

9

"I TELL YOU, Isaiah, I think the whole thing is very odd," Dewey James remarked to her dog. Isaiah, who was accustomed to long disquisitions from his mistress, looked upon her mildly. So far, Dewey hadn't uttered any of the key words—not *dinner* nor *ride* nor even *walk*. Isaiah was not a dog to get worked up about mere trifles; he rested his head in his paws and waited.

This familiar scene was going forth in the kitchen in Dewey's farmhouse, about four miles from the center of town, out on Hillside Road. The house, which was close to two centuries old, had been Dewey's home for forty years, since the first day of her marriage. She gazed out now through the window over the kitchen sink; from here she could see the little red stable that accommodated Starbuck, her seedy but lovable chestnut mare. The horse in question was in the small enclosure in back of the house, sauntering peacefully about in the sunshine, her breath coming up off the frosted grass in enormous billows of early-morning steam. Dewey smiled. She really loved Starbuck.

At any rate, it was a beautiful morning; and Dewey made up her mind to ride over to Marshy Point. While the hunters were out bravely stalking the fearsome doves, she would at least have the benefit of fresh air and sunshine. It would be the perfect way to work up an appetite, too—and Dewey felt certain that George would have outdone himself today. George Farnham packed the best picnic in Hamilton.

She wondered about the gaffe with Cedric. Would the rector take Powell's tactlessness to heart? Well, there was nothing to be done about it now, at any rate. George always said that if people wanted to be nincompoops, there was nothing to be done. Harrison Powell, it turned out, was a nincompoop. Either that or a very deep young man. Like the esthete in *Patience,* thought Dewey. "'Why, what a very singularly deep young man,'" she sang, "'this deep young man must be!'"

Dewey was a little bit surprised, however, at the crowd that was expected out there this morning. With the exception of Bruce Ward, the Marshy Point guide, and George Farnham (whom Powell had invited, Dewey felt sure, for the political clout he wielded in town), it was a churchy group. Dewey began to think she had been unfair to Powell. Perhaps he had invited Cedric only out of a wish not to give offense. It would make sense, after all. And you had to admit that the excursion did sound like fun—for everyone but the birds, Dewey supposed, and if you went in for that kind of thing.

Mary and Sonny Royce, two of Dewey's neighbors and friends, had been invited. And George wanted to go, because Bruce Ward was a friend and a great sportsman. Even Elsie Resnick, the alto soloist, was going. She seemed to have taken quite a liking to young Harrison Powell.

Owen Bennet, of course, would not be there. It was too bad, really, that the men had had such a terrible falling out. If it had been over a woman, Dewey could have understood it; but she really felt it was time they buried the hatchet. Why on earth couldn't they learn to sing a duet or something? Owen Bennet had once been a crack shot, and today's hunt would have been right up his alley, in the old days. Who knows? thought Dewey. He might still be up to the singular challenge of staying sober long enough to try his aim.

Dewey glanced at the clock on the wall. It was nearly ten-thirty; the brave hunters had been out stalking the poor silly birds for hours. Dewey didn't like to think about it.

"Those poor little things, Isaiah," said Dewey—although she had to admit it was difficult to feel sorry for doves. Much easier to pity a mallard or a goose.

But there were occasions when she admired Cedric Hastings for his choices, and this morning was one of them. How much more peaceful life would be if we didn't have to kill our dinner before we ate it, she thought.

Now thoroughly disconcerted by her train of thought, Dewey stood helpless in her kitchen, in front of her open icebox. She had been on the point of making herself some breakfast, but she was momentarily lost in speculation about the grim reality of the food chain. It was dimly possible that even vegetables felt some kind of pain when they were harvested. "Maybe we're just too unsophisticated to comprehend it, Isaiah," she remarked aloud. "It doesn't sound impossible, do you think?"

Her thoughts took her appetite clean away. If one allowed oneself to think this way, she told herself sternly, one would simply have to stop eating altogether. Which was just not practical.

"Time to do something, old boy," she said to the dog, "before I lose all my marbles and begin worrying about whether or not my toast suffers in the toaster."

When things got to be too much for Dewey—which they sometimes did—she often found respite in saddling up Starbuck for a brisk ride. She was glad she had decided to ride over this morning. It would be the perfect excursion.

Dewey James was an able horsewoman, and while she was not in the class with the local professionals, she had ridden to hounds often enough in her day to feel quite at home, galloping away through the fields and pastures of the area. She would take a quick sprint around the old hunt course, and then a detour across Adams Hill to the ducking club.

"You stay here, boy," she said to Isaiah and dashed upstairs to change her clothes.

The Marshy Point Ducking Club was about three miles from Dewey's house, as the crow flies. That morning Dewey fairly flew, pressing Starbuck with unaccustomed urgency across the fields, up over the old brush jumps, and down the winding trail through the woods. The ride took her just over twenty-five minutes; she arrived feeling exalted, concerned only that the Beaujolais would be unfit to drink. They would just have to let it rest a while, she reflected.

One look at the somber group assembled on the front porch, however, told her that they would not be uncorking the wine this noontime.

10

DEWEY'S ATTENTION WAS arrested by the presence of Lisa Nelson, one of the local doctors. She was crouched over an unmoving figure that lay hidden by a blanket. Even under the cover of the blanket, the body had a look of unreality, of life departed. On the porch a half dozen other people stood about awkwardly, frozen in various poses of curiosity, repulsion, and horror. A tableau vivante, thought Dewey inanely. A still life.

Leaning against a porch railing was Mary Royce, a vivacious, dark-haired beauty who was the publisher of the local weekly newspaper, the Hamilton *Quill*. She was dressed in gum boots and a large mud-colored jacket, stained with rust-brown blotches; even from this distance Dewey could see that the stains were still damp. At her side was her husband, Sonny, a large, bearded man, an avid fisherman and sportsman. He was clutching a twelve-gauge shotgun, broken at the middle, its barrels gaping obscenely. Sonny Royce was an experienced hunter; yet he held his gun away from his body in a stiff-armed pose of deep discomfort, almost alienation, as though it were contaminated.

Cecilia Parker, the pert widow from the alto section of the choir, was huddled up next to Bruce Ward, the senior guide. Dewey could tell at a glance that Cecilia had taken special care with her outfit this morning; a pity that its effect would be so lost in the events of the day. She could tell that Cecilia Parker had taken a liking to Bruce Ward.

Ward was a tall man in his middle forties, with blond curls

and blue eyes; an engineer by training, he worked during the week for Mackenzie Munitions—the company that had tried to buy Cedric Hastings's place. On weekends during the season he indulged his passion for the outdoors and brought in a little cash by working as a guide for the Marshy Point Ducking Club. Dewey liked Ward, and under ordinary circumstances would have been very glad to see him.

Elsie Resnick, the alto soloist who had been Harrison Powell's friend and champion in the choir, was off on her own, observing her companions from a position of ten or twelve feet away. To Dewey's eye, Elsie seemed the least upset; her face bore a composed expression of acceptance, and she seemed to be thinking about the situation. Whereas the others, thought Dewey, were still in shock.

Dewey rode up to the front porch and dismounted, breaking the spell that seemed to have been cast over Harrison Powell's assembled guests. As she hurried up the stairs, George Farnham emerged from the old clubhouse, his face grim.

Lisa Nelson stood straight and looked around at the group. "I'm afraid nothing can be done for him."

Dewey approached Elsie Resnick.

"Harrison Powell," said Elsie simply. "He's dead."

Dewey stood still, taking it all in. She glanced at George, who nodded almost imperceptibly.

"When Fielding Booker gets here," said Dr. Nelson, "we'll probably need an account of everyone's movements. But I think we'd better just come clean now." Dr. Nelson was a young woman, but she radiated competence. She had taken control of the situation cleanly and without self-aggrandizement. That was natural; for it was she who had pronounced Harrison Powell's life extinct. By virtue of that simple act she was in charge. "Who fired the shot?"

Everyone looked stunned. Finally Sonny Royce spoke. "There seems to be a problem about that," he said.

"What do you mean, a problem?" asked Dr. Nelson.

Royce scratched his beard and took in a deep breath. "Lisa, listen. It wasn't one of us."

"Then whom do you suggest?" Dr. Nelson stuck to the question. "I know this is a shock, but somebody killed this man."

The little group stood silent. Finally Bruce Ward spoke.

"I heard a noise, from the other side of the cornfield. We were all in that field, walking through in a—in a line. To flush the birds."

"Well, then. Someone must be missing from the group."

"There is nobody missing," said Mary Royce in clipped tones. "We are all here. And we have been together all the morning."

Lisa Nelson looked at each of them. Dewey was impressed by the way the young woman was handling the situation, which called for cool intelligence. "You have nothing to say?"

The hunters shook their heads. George, spotting Dewey, moved to her side and spoke softly to her.

"Hello, my dear. Looks like we'll have to postpone lunch."

Dewey felt her legs go weak. "I had a feeling that something was going to happen."

He cocked an eye at her. "You were right." He lowered his voice. "Very strange, indeed."

"Dear heaven," said Dewey.

"I suggest that we all wait inside," said Lisa Nelson in a tone that required compliance. "Sonny, all of you, put your guns down inside the front door. The police will be here any minute."

The little crowd moved somberly inside the old house. It was colder indoors than out; the clubhouse got little use, except for the annual meeting. It had once been the summer place of the Adams family, a large and merry group of old-time Hamiltonians who had moved away, one by one, until there wasn't a single Adams left in town—although nearly everything was named for them. The house was rather romantic, thought Dewey as she looked around. Her eye took in the crumbling plaster of the ceilings, the mournful empty sconces on the living-room wall, the moth-eaten velvet curtains at the windows, and the seedy old sofas and chairs that the Ducking Club members called "furniture."

Dewey could just barely recall visiting Purnell Adams out here when she was a small child. They had taken turns pushing each other about in a wheelbarrow, while other children tumbled and played under the august oak trees that formed a windbreak along the fields. The Adams family had spent only its summers in the drafty old mansion, preferring their house on Slingluff Avenue, in town, for the winters. The place had been the scene of large and happy family gatherings, with all the cousins and aunts and uncles coming from Indiana and Virginia and even as far away as Maryland to breathe the country air and to while away summer afternoons on the front porch.

The group found seats inside and waited in silence for Fielding Booker's arrival. Although it was Harrison Powell who had perished, Dewey's thoughts and sympathies over the tragedy were with Cedric; which was odd, when she thought of it. But it seemed unfair that he should lose his new young friend so quickly—and in such a manner.

Fielding Booker arrived in short order, accompanied by his young sergeant, Mike Fenton. He nodded briefly at the stricken group and then disappeared with Lisa Nelson for a hurried conference out of earshot in the kitchen.

Booker was a tall man in his late fifties, handsome, with an imposing brow and passion in his gray eyes. He had an old-fashioned admiration for adventure tales and a penchant for the fiery and patriotic poetry of Rudyard Kipling. His knack for sartorial elegance was similarly out of step with the times—he wore beautifully cut and impossibly old-fashioned double-breasted suits, topping them off, more often than not, with an ancient but still fine homburg. He was rather charmingly proud of his good looks and his good taste.

It was commonly assumed in Hamilton that Fielding Booker had once envisioned for himself a life of excitement and glamour as a great, world-class detective. Alas, it was not to be. Booker's intelligence was only limited by his imagination— which was woefully lacking. Here in Hamilton he kept the peace competently enough until it was well and fully disturbed by the commission of an actual crime. Then the great captain of the Hamilton police found himself sadly at sea.

Mike Fenton, Booker's bright-eyed and energetic sergeant, was this morning charged with keeping an eye on the group in the living room. As he took up a watchful position near the door to the hall, Fenton permitted himself a smile for Dewey.

Fenton was loyal to his superior; but there was loyalty, and then there was loyalty. He had heard enough from Lisa Nelson to comprehend that this was no ordinary hunting accident that had taken the life of Harrison Powell. And, when it came right down to it, he knew—like everyone else in Hamilton—that his superior would probably need a few pointers in the matter of finding the truth. As likely as not, it would be dotty old Dewey James who furnished him with his clues and provided him with the answer to the problem at hand.

Dewey James had by now quite a reputation in Hamilton as an amateur sleuth; for she was curious—interfering, some might have said—and she was unafraid of confronting the facts as she saw them. In situations such as this one, Fielding Booker didn't welcome Dewey's help, but Mike Fenton knew that the captain would be lost without it. Fenton reminded himself to buy his chief a large bottle of antacid. Dewey James had that kind of effect on Fielding Booker.

Booker emerged from his consultation with Lisa Nelson and spoke to the group. "I'm going to need statements from everyone, and I hope you will cooperate. It is apparent to me that this tragedy is not an accident, and I must ask your forbearance if you find my questions irritating." He looked sternly around at the group. "Successful police work is very much the product of a dedication to sifting through details, which may be tiresome for you. Now—Dr. Nelson has told me that all of you were invited here this morning for some shooting. Doves, was it, Sonny?"

Sonny Royce, thus appealed to, nodded.

"All of you?"

"Er, well . . ." began Mary Royce, with a look at Dewey. "Yes, Mary?"

Dewey plunged in. "I wasn't one of the shooting party, Bookie. I merely, well, happened to come by."

"Oh." Booker's face was an unreadable mask. "At what time did you happen to drop by, Dewey?"

"Just a few moments before you arrived. I was coming to have lunch with everyone."

A look of relief, evident to all, crossed Booker's face. Mike Fenton knew the source of the relief; so did Dewey, although she did not mean to be left out of things quite so easily. Booker shifted his gaze politely to the rest of the group.

"I am going to ask each of you to surrender your weapon to my sergeant; I hope there will be no objection?"

The group shook their heads. "Good," said Booker, feeling in control. He was in his element now. "This deserted house is no place for the police to conduct their inquiries," he went on. "If you will all be good enough to accompany me back to

town, to headquarters, we can begin to take your statements.''
He smiled at Dewey. ''All excepting you, ma'am, since you
were not here at the time.''

George winked at Dewey. He would fill her in, she knew,
later on in the day.

To Fielding Booker's amazement, therefore, Dewey calmly
assented to his directive. She took a quiet leave of the group,
mounted Starbuck, and headed home across the fields. The day
had warmed, but there was a storm brewing in the east as she
made her way slowly and thoughtfully back through the woods
and across the green pastures. She had several ideas racing
through her head, but the first thing she wanted to do was to see
Cedric Hastings. He ought to learn about Harrison Powell from
someone he knew, she reflected. And Dewey was curious to
see how Cedric Hastings would take it. You never knew, really,
how he took things. All in all, Cedric Hastings was an odd
duck.

11

CHARLOTTE HASTINGS OPENED her kitchen door and looked at Dewey with interest.

"Mrs. James?"

"Charlotte. I must speak to you. Is Cedric here?"

"Come in, Mrs. James." Charlotte led the way into the kitchen. After two years in the role Charlotte had learned the ropes of filling in for Cedric when members of the parish came looking for him. But Dewey James, in the ordinary course of things, didn't seek Cedric out for advice and consolation. The sturdy librarian was not made that way. "I'm afraid he's out," Charlotte continued. "Old Mrs. Hatfield again. This time it's her rheumatism." She reached instinctively for the teakettle and filled it, gesturing Dewey to a seat at the kitchen table. "Is there something I can do for you?"

"Well," Dewey began, taking a deep breath. "I've got some dreadful news, I'm afraid. There was an accident this morning at the Marshy Point Ducking Club. Harrison Powell is dead."

Charlotte's hand froze in midair, the kettle poised above the lighted burner.

"No," she said simply. She breathed in slowly and deeply, then set the kettle down on the burner very quietly and joined Dewey at the table. "You'd better tell me about it."

"Yes, I suppose I had better. Well—to begin with, you must have known about the little shooting party he had arranged for this morning." Dewey studied Charlotte's face carefully. The young woman nodded, and her eyes filled with tears.

"Oh, yes. We knew all about it." Her voice contained a sadness and a bitterness that Dewey hadn't anticipated. Perhaps Cedric had been insulted by the young man's lack of sensitivity. Perhaps, after all, Dewey had been right about that.

Dewey went on. "There really isn't much to tell—and I don't know enough about such parties to give you a clear picture. But the plan was to form a large semicircle and move forward through the north field—you know, behind the apple orchard." Charlotte nodded and Dewey continued. "They were trying to flush the birds, you see, beforehand. They took up their positions in the field and began to walk forward. The birds flew up, and someone got off a shot from the opposite side. Only it went wrong."

"Dear heaven," murmured Charlotte, looking at Dewey in horror. "Who did it?"

Dewey shook her head. There was no point, just now, of going into the intricacies of the matter. It would all be common knowledge within a few hours, but Dewey sidestepped. "I don't know. No one is certain, just yet. But I thought you ought to hear about it right away, which is why I came by. I hope you don't mind."

The kettle began to boil, screaming out its shrill alarm. Charlotte paid no attention, so Dewey rose and turned the flame off. The parrot, in his cage in the corner, began to squawk noisily, emitting unintelligible and fragmented syllables. The bird, as everyone in town knew, spoke only ancient Greek. How did Charlotte put up with it? wondered Dewey, as she rummaged in the cabinets for tea and sugar. The young woman seemed not to notice the rising noise level in the little room. One got used to things, thought Dewey, as she brewed a pot of good, strong, hot tea.

"Here you go, my child," she said, putting a mug down before her. "What time will Cedric be home?"

Charlotte roused herself as though from a dream. "Oh. Cedric." She looked at her watch. "He should be here any minute."

"Where's Ben?"

"Ellen Fenton took him this morning—I needed to be out and about." Charlotte seemed to revive. "I suppose I should be grateful for a morning off," she said with a smile, sipping at her tea. "But I miss the little monster."

"Charlotte—I don't want to pry, you know," Dewey began.

Charlotte Hastings waved aside Dewey's polite demurral. Dewey James was well known for her love of getting to the bottom of things. A month ago Charlotte would have closed the topic, out of loyalty to Cedric. But all of a sudden Charlotte didn't mind so much. "Pry, by all means, Mrs. James. And when you've got all the facts, you can fill me in."

"Well, it just struck me that there was something altogether too intense about that young man. Deliberate."

Charlotte nodded. "Deliberate. That's a good word for it, Mrs. James."

"Yes. I suppose it is. And—well, you have to admit, it was strange, the way he turned up here on your doorstep."

"Out of nowhere." Charlotte nodded vigorously. "He just arrived. And kind of took over our lives, for a time."

"I must say I think you were rather good about it. He stayed here for—how long? Six weeks?"

"Six weeks and two days," said Charlotte with a flash of acerbic humor. "And then he moved into Cedric's house."

"Yes."

Slowly, and with great dignity, Charlotte Hastings began to weep. Her tears rolled quietly down her cheeks, and she looked at Dewey without a trace of embarrassment at thus revealing herself. "I'm a little sorry, now, that I wasn't kinder to him," she said.

"Because you told Cedric you had had enough."

"That's right." Charlotte wiped away a tear. "I said it was too much, with the baby, to have a houseguest for so long. Cedric said he wasn't a guest, he was a friend in need. But I finally put my foot down."

"And that was when Cedric thought of selling him the house?"

"Oh—no." Charlotte looked surprised. "That happened ages before. Almost the minute that Harrison Powell walked through the front door."

As they drank their tea, Charlotte told the story, such as it was. While she talked, the parrot shuffled noisily in his cage, emitting an occasional fragment of mumbo jumbo. Charlotte told Dewey about how Harrison Powell had seemed to work some kind of magic with Cedric. The clergyman had at first been delighted by the young man's visit; they had stayed up late into the night, three nights running, looking over the old pictures of Powell's parents from the Kerangani days. Cedric had told wonderfully amusing stories about their exploits—all kinds of stories, about the little village and its people, about fishing for Nile perch in the lake, and learning to snorkel in the Indian Ocean, about their visits to the Serengeti Plain to see the lions and the cheetah and the elephants.

But then, Charlotte said, something shifted. "I don't know how to explain it," she said. "One night, when Cedric came to bed, he seemed disturbed. I asked him what was troubling him, but he didn't want to discuss it. Said that I was imagining things."

"Ah," said Dewey, who was familiar with the ways of husbands and wives. "And so you left it alone."

"Yes, I did," said Charlotte. "Frankly, I thought that perhaps he didn't much like Harrison after those first few days, but felt it would be disloyal to say so. Harrison is—was—the kind of person who just walks in and takes over. On the other hand, I considered the possibility that *we* were somehow in Cedric's way. Ben and I."

"Oh, dear."

Charlotte smiled and shook back her thick locks of red-brown hair, her eyes flashing. "Now, that was pretty stupid, I admit. But you know how things can just occur to you—silly things that don't mean anything. And Cedric had been a bachelor for so long, you know."

"Yes, indeed, I know."

"And then there came the night of the dinner party. After that everything seemed to be different."

Dewey sat back and listened, deeply interested. Charlotte went on.

"We had just the usual suspects—you know, Julia, Wally—who else? Oh, Cecilia Parker, of course, for Wally. Or Wally for Cecilia. And Harrison seemed to—well, to go to work on them. I can't explain it. Wally asked him to join the church choir. But I felt almost as though he was trying to sell us all on something. Does that make any sense at all, Mrs. James?"

"Indeed it does," murmured Dewey. That young man had been selling them all on himself. Dewey remembered the way

he had charmed her, that first day when she had given him a lift
to the rectory. He had been smooth, and quite believable. But
there had been something about it that had not rung true.
Dewey thought hard for a moment. The situation seemed
fraught with possibilities.

"And that was the night," continued Charlotte, "that we
first talked about the house. Cecilia Parker thought we'd never
find a buyer, and Julia and Cedric were laughing about the old
place. Harrison was interested, and so the following day Cedric
took him out there. The next thing I knew, we had found
someone to take it off our hands."

"Charlotte," Dewey said, "I wonder. Would you mind if I
had a look through those pictures?"

"Pictures?"

"The ones from Kerangani."

Charlotte, surprised, was quick to oblige. She went to the
den and reappeared a few moments later with an old shoebox
of photos. She sifted through them rapidly and found one of
Harrison Powell's parents. "That's Dan Powell, and there's his
wife, Lucy. Cedric took that one. I always had the impression
he had lived in some mud hut over there, but just look at the
house."

Dewey looked. It was a large, rambling stone structure, with
cheerful, red-framed windows, a red tile roof, and a huge bank
of carefully tended bougainvillea framing it.

Charlotte pulled out another. "Here's one of Cedric. Look at
all that blond hair!"

Dewey studied the man in the photograph. She remembered
Cedric well from those days; he had been full of exultation,
ready to take the world by storm. He was uncompromising,
then as now; but there was something in his expression, in this
picture, that was at odds with the hermitlike young cleric that
Dewey had known. Perhaps it was the suntan; or the cloud of
pink in the background. She looked closely at the picture while
Charlotte explained.

"He and Lucy went out to Lake Makuna or Turkapi or
Something-or-other to look at flamingos. They got their car
stuck in the mud, and they had to push it out. Just look at those
flamingos."

Yes, indeed, thought Dewey. There was an unexpected
quality to this photo of Cedric Hastings. He seemed to possess

a secret knowledge, a quiet happiness, that to Dewey seemed at odds with the man she had known for sixty-odd years.

Dewey looked up at Charlotte, who nodded. "I think he must have been in love with her. Which would explain a lot."

Yes, indeed, thought Dewey. That would explain a great deal. Deeply disturbed, she took her leave of Charlotte.

12

In his small, overfurnished office at the Hamilton police station, Fielding Booker was in a snit.

He had spent the last four hours deeply immersed in his investigation of Harrison Powell's death. He had interviewed all the witnesses, with the exception of George Farnham, whom he was saving for last. Every one of them was certain that the fatal shot had not been fired by one of their number. Booker was foxed; if he couldn't budge them, he couldn't find out who had done the deed. The ballistics report would be in by tomorrow morning; but Booker wasn't certain it would help.

Robert Gaston, the county medical examiner, had sent over his report on the wound. The shell that had killed Powell had contained not ordinary shot, but double-buck—a powerful sort of ammunition that was sometimes used in deer season. The deer season in Hamilton had been over for a week. And Fielding Booker, who had been raised in the country, knew that no one in his right mind went after a mourning dove with a shell holding four balls of lead, each the size of a marble. The only thing that remained was to discover which of the six persons at the dove shoot had been loaded for bear.

A preliminary examination of all the weapons showed that none of them had contained a shell of double-buck. But with all the commotion it would be easy enough to substitute a new shell while everyone looked the other way.

"Mikey, this is bad news, I'm afraid," he said to his sergeant.

"Yessir."

"What we've got here, Mike my boy, is a plain case of reckless endangerment. But we have to shake them up a bit, my boy."

"Sir."

"Did you get on to the state wildlife boys yet?"

"Yessir. Everyone's license was in order, duck stamps, dove permit, everything. No problem there."

"Doves are federally protected, Mike. I hope to heaven we don't get the feds on this one, muddying the waters for us."

"No, sir."

"Find out anything about their weapons?"

"Not yet, sir. But Kate should have it before long." Kate Shoemaker was one of two rookie officers on the town force. She had proved herself an able policewoman, but Booker still harbored an archaic sense that women and crime didn't mix. It was typical of him; and it was just one of the unfortunate blind spots that had held him back from a great career in law enforcement.

"Are you sure she'll, ah, do for the job, Mikey?"

"Yessir."

Booker grumbled. "All right, then. I'll see George Farnham now."

Fenton departed to the main waiting room, and a few moments later George Farnham appeared in Booker's office.

"Sit down, George, please." Booker regarded the lawyer somberly. This wasn't going to be easy. Fielding Booker knew that George Farnham had the power to make the next few days—or weeks, if the investigation took so long—a waking misery for him. Anything that was said in this office, Booker knew, would be reported straight to Dewey James.

Fielding Booker liked Dewey James, was fond of her. She was, after all, the widow of his former superior officer on the force. And Brendan James had been a damned respectable police officer. Booker would be the first to acknowledge it. But his widow was something else again. Now that she had retired—or semiretired—from her job at the library, she seemed to be hankering after some kind of second career on the force. Women! thought Booker, shaking his head. They could never leave anything alone. His first order of business, therefore, was to lay down the law with George Farnham. Dewey

James was to be kept far away from this business—and well out of Booker's hair.

"First things first, George," said Booker, as the lawyer took a seat. "I'm sure I don't have to tell you that the proceedings of this investigation are to remain absolutely confidential."

"Oh?"

"Yes." Booker glowered at Farnham. "George," he went on in a milder tone, "I know that you and Dewey are friends. Close friends. And I know that she has been—er, rather helpful over one or two details in recent cases here. However, I don't want any meddle—help on this one. The facts are absolutely straightforward. All I need is your cooperation. I want you to tell me who fired that shot."

Farnham shifted comfortably in his chair. He liked Fielding Booker, rather a lot. But he wasn't about to make any rash promises. Besides, it would do no good—the way the Hamilton grapevine worked, there wasn't a chance that Dewey wouldn't hear all about it, one way or another.

"Bookie, let's forget the personalities involved, for the moment. You know as well as I do that I haven't got a chance of stemming the flow of information, once it starts."

Booker waved it away. "Forget it, then. Suppose we start at the beginning. You tell me what was going on out there this morning. A little shooting party, eh? Like England, or on some heath or something. What—the fellow thought you were the aristocracy, eh? Decided to butter you up."

George chuckled. Booker's take on the situation neatly coincided with his own, as it happened. "You're right, there, Bookie," he agreed. "Harrison Powell was working to establish himself in this town. Joined the church, joined the choir, bought the Hastings place, and went hunting with the boys."

"Yes," grumbled Booker. "Then, bang, he's dead. I want to know who was responsible for the accident, George. No whitewashing. I won't have a coverup in Hamilton."

Farnham shook his head. "It wasn't one of us, Bookie. Only two shots were fired from the line, my own and Mary Royce's. I was watching Mary at the time, and I know she was aiming for the birds. Have you considered other possibilities?"

Booker gave Farnham a disappointed look. "You, too, George? Please. Out with it."

"But that's the truth, Bookie. Look." He turned a pad of

paper toward him and picked up a pencil. In a few quick motions he had sketched the lay of the land at Marshy Point—the old house at the center, the woods to the east running down to the river, and the cornfields running west to another small, marshy area. "Ever hunted dove, Bookie?"

"No."

"Well—here's how it was going to work. We arranged ourselves in a line, about twenty yards apart, and moved slowly up through the corn stubble. When we got to about here"—he marked a place that was opposite the beginning of the northern extension of the woods—"we flushed some birds. Now, doves fly erratically, not straight. They burst up out of the ground, then kind of zigzag. Which is what they did this morning.

"I got off the first shot, then I heard Mary Royce's gun go off. She was next to me. Sonny and Elsie were next, then Ward, then Powell. Closest to the cover of the woods."

"Where was Cecilia Parker?"

"She was off to the left, near the clubhouse. She doesn't hunt, and we didn't think it would be a good idea to have her anywhere too close."

"No, I see that," said Booker with feeling. He didn't particularly care for the widow Parker; she made him nervous.

Farnham went on. "I heard another shot, from next to the woods. I thought it must have come from Powell, but when I looked around, I couldn't see him. The others must have noticed at the same time, because we all began to run toward him."

"And when you got there?"

"When we got there, he was dying. He lasted about no more than a couple of minutes, I'd say—though it would be hard to judge it absolutely accurately. There was a lot of commotion. Mary Royce, of course, kept her head. She applied pressure to the wound, but there was nothing to be done."

"But you weren't actually watching the others, George. You couldn't swear that none of them got off that shot. How about Elsie Resnick? She was close enough."

Farnham nodded. "I did think at first that it must have been Elsie—she was the only one with a clear field toward him, and the only one close enough. But when I saw that wound, I knew it couldn't have been her."

"Oh?"

"That's right. First of all, she was ahead of him, and he was shot in the back. Second, she was shooting with a four-ten. Wouldn't have done the same kind of damage." Farnham leaned in closer to Booker, studying him carefully across the desk. "In fact, Bookie, it looked to me as though it might have been the work of a powerful rifle—except it didn't sound like a rifle. Sounded like a twelve-gauge."

Booker stirred in his chair. It was looking, more and more, like a case of premeditated murder. He picked up Robert Gaston's report and glanced through it quickly, then turned Farnham's drawing around to study it more closely. "Sonny Royce said he heard some kind of noise. Coming from about here." He pointed to a spot just at the edge of the field, where the shrubby understory began. "You think it's possible there was someone there, George?"

"I do."

Booker nodded. There was a knock at his office door, and Kate Shoemaker appeared. She was a lively young woman, good looking and competent. George Farnham, who knew her parents well, nodded to her.

"I have the report on all the weapons present at the scene, sir," said Officer Shoemaker, tendering a piece of paper. She glanced uncomfortably at Farnham. "Everything is in order. The registrations, that is, sir."

"Bring it on, girl," said Booker querulously. "No need to make a mystery of it." He stuck out a hand for the paper. "Now we'll get to the bottom of this."

While Booker's attention was thus absorbed, Farnham stole a look at the medical examiner's report. Like most people endowed with a healthy share of curiosity, George Farnham was skilled at reading upside down. He glanced down the report quickly and saw immediately that his suspicions had been right. The shell that killed Powell had contained no ordinary bird shot.

Fielding Booker caught George in the act. He hastily put away the medical report.

"Thank you for your help, George." Booker dismissed him.

As George Farnham made his way out the front door of the little brick building, he thought about the report from the medical examiner. There had been but one box of shells out at the Hastings place this morning, supplied by Bruce Ward. He was pretty sure that Ward knew his shot; it would be unlikely that he had allowed such a careless error to be made. But it was always a possibility that someone had brought his own shells. Or her own.

George Farnham shook his head. No, the person who had pulled the trigger was not one of their small group. Sonny Royce and Bruce Ward had both heard a noise from the woods. George Farnham would be willing to swear that the noise they had heard was the murderer, making his escape.

13

"So," said MIRABELLE Meissen, in her clipped Swiss accent, looking about her with a smirk. "Today our Julia gives us chocolate chips."

Mirabelle's fellow choir members snubbed this conversational gambit. Most of them had long ago given up trying to have a civilized conversation with her; for no matter what the subject, she was sure to remind them of the superiority of the Swiss way of doing things. Chocolate chips, as everyone knew, were a topic to be avoided at the best of times; and this Saturday afternoon certainly didn't qualify as the best of times.

Wally Penberry had rounded up the choir for an emergency rehearsal; there was just time to work up a new anthem for the church service tomorrow morning. Given the events of the day, Wally felt that his setting of Psalm 94 (with the tenor solo, "They slay the widow and the stranger, and murder the fatherless") would not do. By now—it was four o'clock—the word had spread like wildfire that Harrison Powell, the fatherless stranger in their midst, had died a violent death.

Julia Boucher stood in her customary spot behind a card table in the common room, pouring out tea and coffee to the choir members and passing the cookies. Arthur Garrison smiled at her as he helped himself to a cookie. It was typical of Julia to realize that they would need the calm reassurance of this ritual before rehearsing. Julia really was a wonder.

Elsie Resnick was sitting alone across the room, her customary buoyancy replaced by an unwonted stillness. She was soon joined by Cecilia Parker, who looked pale and shaken. The morning's episode had forged a bond of sorts between them; the rest of the singers, fully aware of the circumstances, chattered in quiet voices, reluctant to intrude.

Undeterred by the pall that had settled over the choir, Mirabelle Meissen plowed ahead. "Anyway, he had a nice voice, that boy," she remarked to Judy Stebbins. "It was even a good voice, but it needed to be trained. I suppose it is too bad he is dead." She reached over and selected the largest cookie from Julia's plate, looked at it disdainfully, then took a large bite.

"At any rate," responded Judy in a low voice, "it doesn't seem to have hurt your appetite."

"Why should it?" Mirabelle said with a frown, her mouth full.

The two women had never much cared for each other, but Judy had always, in the past, been careful to keep her dislike under wraps. This afternoon, however, Mirabelle looked to be going too far.

"Have a heart, Mirabelle," said Judy. "Just can it, all right?"

"Ho! 'Can it.' You know what I think? He wouldn't be dead if there wasn't some reason. People don't just get themselves killed off for nothing, you know, even in America."

You had to hand it to Mirabelle. Lacking any sort of native tact to keep her wandering thoughts in check, she gave voice to the conclusion that they had all began to reach. There was a deep uneasiness among the singers; even the most tactful of them were suspicious.

Wally Penberry clapped his hands together and motioned the choir to follow him. Quietly they obeyed, filing up the stairs to the music room, leaving Julia Boucher to dispose of the coffee cups and put away the leftover chocolate-chip cookies.

As Julia bustled about, she could hear their voices drifting down the stairwell, and she nodded to herself. Wally had made a good selection, his own setting of the first letter of Paul to the Corinthians: "Behold, I show you a mystery: we shall not all sleep, but we shall all be changed. . . . For the trumpet shall sound, and the dead shall be raised incorruptible. . . . O death, where is thy sting? O grave, where is thy victory?"

* * *

At about the same moment George Farnham was taking his leave of Fielding Booker at the police station. He headed straight for Dewey's place, feeling no compunction. It was all very well for Fielding Booker to want to keep his investigation to himself, but the one little fact that George had gleaned made him realize, instantly, that this situation might be tricky. He wanted to talk it over with Dewey, for the good of them all.

Dewey greeted her old friend with some impatience; it had been many hours now since Fielding Booker had sent her packing from the scene of the crime, and after her visit to Charlotte Hastings, Dewey had gone home to stew. Dewey James did not like to sit on the sidelines.

"George! Where in heaven's name have you been? I've been waiting to hear from you for hours."

"Cooling my heels, my dear. Cooling my heels and being interrogated by our local constabulary." He took off his coat and plunked himself down familiarly at Dewey's kitchen table.

Dewey smiled. She knew Booker's style of interrogation rather well. "A policeman's lot is not an 'appy one, George."

"I suppose not," he conceded. "But now, my dear, I am ready to make a full report to the real brains of this town."

Dewey made them a pot of coffee as George told his tale. She made him start at the beginning and describe once more the scene in the cornfield.

"You're certain you heard the shot, George? Oh, how dreadful."

Farnham nodded, his face careworn. "I didn't care much for that young fella, I have to admit. Still—someone shot him in the back, Dewey." He shook his head and looked grimly at his old friend. "Bookie has the impression that one of us out there did it. But I would be willing to swear that the shot came from the other side of the field, from the woods. Sonny Royce thought he heard some kind of noise in the woods. But we were all so concerned with that young fella that we didn't pay attention to anything else."

"No one could blame you for that," said Dewey kindly. It was plain that George felt he had slipped up; he was worried by the thought that he should have been more on top of things. "Bookie can't seriously think that any one of you would do such a thing without owning up to it. After all, accidents do happen.''

"This was no accident, Dewey.'' He gave her a serious look. "I managed to get a quick look at the report that the medical examiner sent over. The shot was all wrong.''

"Whatever do you mean?''

"The shot. It wasn't the kind of shell you would use for dove, my dear. It was what they call double-buck—big, round balls, like bullets. Designed for bigger game.''

"Heavens!'' Dewey was shocked. "You mean to say this whole thing was premeditated?''

"Looks that way. Unless I am very much mistaken, we have a cold-blooded killer on the loose in Hamilton.''

Dewey sat lost in thought. It was inconceivable to her that Harrison Powell had managed to find a deadly enemy in the two short months he had lived in Hamilton. She voiced her doubts to George.

"Well,'' Farnham pointed out reasonably, "he managed to get into a fistfight at the Seven Locks the other day. Nils Reichart told me all about it.''

"With whom?''

"Bennet.''

"Oh.'' She looked at George inquiringly. "You don't think that Owen Bennet—?''

"Don't know what to think. He's a hothead, that Bennet. And mean, when he takes a drink.''

"Yes,'' Dewey agreed.

"And, Dewey—he used to be the president of the Marshy Point Ducking Club. He's quite a shot.''

"Dear God,'' murmured Dewey as she began to see the possibilities. That Owen Bennet was capable of bad behavior, she would readily acknowledge. But she wondered: Was he capable of planning and carrying out a murder? Murder seemed an extreme course of action, even for a hotheaded tenor.

Besides—it simply didn't add up. There was something in the whole situation that didn't add up. There must be something more.

"George—what did we really know about that young man?''

"Not much,'' George admitted. "Cedric knows more than anyone, I'd guess.''

"Yes. Yes, he does." She thought back to her conversation with Charlotte Hastings. "George, I went to see Cedric this morning. After I got home from that place—I thought it would be the right thing to do, to tell Cedric in person. Before he heard it through the rumor mill."

"Oh? That was good of you, Dewey. How did he take the news?"

"He wasn't there. But I had a very interesting talk with Charlotte. George—I think there is something about this whole thing that we don't know yet. Something secret, buried."

"You do?" George was intrigued.

"I do. George, I'm going to talk to Cedric tomorrow. I have a feeling he hasn't been quite honest with the good people of Hamilton."

14

FIELDING BOOKER WAS out of sorts. He had not counted on this kind of complication; when he had set out this morning, in answer to Lisa Nelson's urgent summons, he had fully expected to have matters wrapped up by midafternoon. But darkness was falling, and suddenly Booker realized that he was confronting something worse, far worse, than a mere hunting accident.

This was the second such aggravation in a week. The first had been the report, received only two days before, of the theft of money from the Church of the Good Shepherd. The information had come to him in a rather roundabout way—through Wally Penberry, who had come, reluctantly, as an emissary from Cedric or Julia. Booker shook his head as he thought about it. Why on earth hadn't those people come to him sooner? A full five days after the crime, the trail—if the thief had left one—was icy cold. Fielding Booker had begun to feel that his competence as captain of police might be called to question if this kind of thing kept up.

"Fenton!" he bellowed.

The young sergeant appeared instantly. "Sir."

"I think we may have a problem."

"Sir?"

"Stop with the sirs, Mikey, and come in and sit down."

Fenton obeyed, making himself comfortable. The old man had a tiger by the tail; Fenton reminded himself to call home and tell his wife he'd be late for supper.

Booker glared at him. "I don't like this, Mike. That double-buck had to come from somewhere, but all those choir-singing clowns swear it wasn't theirs."

"Yes, sir."

"Now, Elsie Resnick—she might have made that kind of mistake, being a woman and everything. But she was shooting a four-ten, too small for that shell."

"Yes, sir."

"Mary Royce's gun had been fired once, but everything looked to be in order there. She seems to know what she's doing, but then, she's got Sonny to show her."

"That's right, sir." Fenton suppressed a smile. Mary Royce was a crack shot, as everyone in town knew. She had won the Marshy Point skeet-shoot three years running.

"George was the only other person who fired. Between you and me, Mikey, George is out of it. I just can't see him being too yellow to own up."

"No, sir. Plus—there was the range. Mr. Farnham was seventy or eighty yards from Powell. With all the others in between. And, sir—they would have noticed if George had done it."

Booker sighed and leaned back heavily in his chair. "I suppose you're right." He thought for a bit, then sat up straight, his gray eyes full of intensity. "Good. Don't like to exclude suspects just because they're my friends, you know. It wouldn't be right."

"No, sir."

"Now, that guide fellow—Bruce Ward—swears he brought a brand-new box of shells out there with him today. That doesn't mean that one of the hunting party couldn't have slipped another shell out of his pocket. But look at it, Mikey."

"Yes, sir."

"That's right. We've got George Farnham's statement that there were only two shots fired before that fatal one. He was watching everyone. Cecilia Parker was too far away to see with any accuracy, but she swears nobody in that group fired at Powell. But she didn't see him fall. She was watching the damned birds."

"Yes, sir."

"Mike, we're going to have to comb that cornfield. One of them must have ejected that shell casing."

"You think so, sir?" Fenton looked out the window; evening was falling. "The light will be a problem."

"I know, I know. Luckily you are young and your eyesight is good. Get Shoemaker and Machen. And I want you to go round to see Jamie Vickers. See what he has in the way of floodlights that he can lend us."

"Right away, sir."

Darkness had begun to settle in earnest when Booker and his three junior officers arrived back at the old ducking club. With them was Jamie Vickers, owner of a local farm-equipment shop, who had brought with him a truck-mounted generator and four powerful floodlights. Vickers was only too glad to help; he was a great chum of Mike Fenton's and was known to be a little sweet on Officer Kate Shoemaker. He rigged up the lights in no time, then stood back to watch.

Armed with the map of the hunt that George Farnham had drawn, Fielding Booker had no trouble reconstructing the events of the morning. But it was cold and damp in the cornfield, and the stubble of the corn sent little spikes through the socks of the search party. The expended shell would be difficult to find, Booker knew; but he was determined not to rest until he found it.

They went over and over the ground, in a sweeping network of searching eyes and probing hands. But after a long hour they had nothing to show for their work.

Finally Josh Machen, the youngest member of the Hamilton force, spoke up. "Sir?"

"What is it, Machen?"

"About the, er, noise, sir, from the woods." Josh Machen had a date for tonight. He wanted to wrap this up. "The noise that Sonny Royce heard."

"Yes?"

"I only wondered if it might be worth a look, being, sir, as we didn't find anything so far."

Booker glowered at the young officer, as much for his flat-footed way of talking as for the audacity of his suggestion. The fruitless search, however, had left Booker no other option, except to return at dawn and try once more. "All right. Fifteen minutes, no more."

The young man took up a flashlight and moved off into the

scrubby understory at the edge of the cornfield. Within minutes the rest of the search party heard his shout.

They raced across the field in answer to Machen's call. He hadn't gone very far into the woods—a mere ten yards or so. But the cover here was dense enough to hide a man who wished to conceal himself.

Machen pointed his flashlight beam downward. "There, sir."

Booker looked. A glint of metal shone up weakly in the flashlight beam. He advanced a few cautious steps and peered closely. "By gum, Machen."

"Thank you, sir."

"You've found it."

"Yeah." Machen grinned.

"Mikey—" Booker turned to his sergeant, struggling to keep the excitement out of his voice. "Careful now, son. Don't let's spoil the prints."

Fenton stepped in, pulling on his gloves, and reached down into the wild sucker growth of an old raspberry bush. Gingerly he extracted the find. It was a twelve-gauge shotgun, beautifully made, with a solid walnut butt and well-tended, carefully oiled barrels.

Kate Shoemaker let out a whistle.

"Well, troops," said Booker, "unless I'm very much mistaken, it looks like we've got a murder on our hands."

15

ON THE SUNDAY following Harrison Powell's death, Cedric Hastings preached to a standing-room-only crowd. Ordinarily, church attendance was much lower (whether because of the failings of its congregation or of its clergy it is difficult to say); but that morning, at least, many laissez-faire worshipers answered an uncommonly strong urge to hear Cedric's sermon.

The good rector did not disappoint them. Last night he had put aside a lengthy disquisition on the vicissitudes of lust and devoted himself to composing a substitute sermon. It was a poignant tribute to the young man who had so briefly been a part of their church and community.

Dewey James had to admit that she was rather catch-as-catch-can in the matter of weekly worship. But this morning she particularly wanted to talk to Cedric, and she knew that the best place to catch him would be in the common room immediately after the service. Thus, it was to the Church of the Good Shepherd that she bent her steps.

Cedric read to them from Psalm 77: "'I call to remembrance my song in the night: I commune with mine own heart: and my spirit made diligent search.'" Then he spoke eloquently of the young stranger who had come into their midst, an orphan and a wanderer, communing with his own heart in his search for a home among them.

"In the day of his trouble he sought the Lord," intoned Cedric, in round and perfect tones. "He gifted us with his song. He came to us a stranger, searching with a diligent spirit, and he lifted his voice in song with us. He made us his home, after his wanderings, and in the dark night of the spirit he sang to us.''

Dewey, listening attentively from a pew in the rear, thought perhaps Cedric had gone a bit far. But the rest of the congregation was moved; and by the time the choir rose to sing its anthem, there wasn't a dry eye in the house.

Dewey caught up with Cedric in the common room after the service.

"Ah, good morning, Dewey," said the good rector, evidently pleased that she had attended.

"Hello, Cedric." She looked at him sympathetically. "That was a very inspiring sermon."

"Thank you, thank you." Cedric generally thought his own sermons inspiring, but the extra effort last night had certainly paid off this morning. He glanced around at the red-eyed worshipers who had come in to the common room for coffee and biscuits. "Will you join us in taking a little refreshment this morning?"

"Oh—no, thank you. Cedric—I wondered if I might have a word with you?"

"Certainly, Dewey."

She glanced around. "Perhaps we could find somewhere a little more private?"

"If you like." They moved off toward a small chapel that was chiefly used for baptisms, and seated themselves in a quiet corner.

"Cedric," said Dewey, feeling at a loss, "I don't quite know how to put this to you."

"Perhaps I can help?" He smiled at her quizzically, his smooth, pallid features glowing strangely in the dim light. "I imagine you'd like to talk to me about Harrison Powell."

"That's right," said Dewey, inhaling deeply and taking the plunge. "Cedric—is there something about that boy that we should know?"

Cedric smiled a thin smile and looked at her with patient resignation. "I very much doubt it."

"Well, you see—I just thought it was odd, the way he sought you out."

"Seemed perfectly natural to me. I was a dear friend of his father."

"And his mother," said Dewey, feeling brave.

"Yes, and his mother," admitted Cedric. "But Lucy has been dead for seventeen years. And it wasn't the same sort of friendship, you know."

"No." Dewey looked him straight in the eye. "I didn't suppose it was."

"In fact, you might say Lucy and I hardly knew each other, after Kerangani."

"Is that right?"

"But I kept up with Dan. We had several interests in common, you know—matters of theology. There were points of disagreement between us, naturally—we were intellectual adversaries of a sort, constantly renewing ourselves on the field of battle."

"Hmm. Do you know, I had the impression that you and Dan Powell had lost touch."

"Lost touch?" Cedric laughed aloud. "Hardly. We wrote each other at least once a month for more than twenty years."

"Was Harrison very like him?"

The question clearly surprised Hastings. "In what way?"

"Well—I don't mean in looks, so much. Because one could see from the pictures that he really looked more like Lucy. All that golden hair."

"Yes," said Hastings, an odd light showing in his eyes. "So you have seen the pictures."

"Charlotte showed them to me yesterday. I asked her to."

"I see. So why ask me, if you have seen for yourself?"

"I want to know if Harrison was like his father in other ways—in personality, in his gestures. And so forth."

"What on earth are you driving at, Dewey?" Hastings rounded on her, annoyance playing over his quiet features.

"I don't really know, Cedric," she said soothingly. "It is just that I wondered, you know, at his having become one of the family, more or less. And so quickly, too."

"We liked each other," said Hastings snappishly. "It was as simple as that." He had closed the subject. "And now, Dewey, if you'll pardon me, I must prepare for the vestry meeting." He rose.

"Oh, yes—go right ahead." She stood. "Cedric, I hope I haven't offended you."

"Offended me? Not in the least. You merely surprise me, Dewey."

Full of misgivings, she watched him go. Then, with only a momentary trepidation of her heart, she headed out through the church for the police station. It was time she and Bookie had a little talk.

"Sunday's supposed to be the day of rest, Dewey," said Booker with a sigh as she appeared at his office door. "So why don't *you* give it a rest?"

There was not much hope in Fielding Booker's voice. This development was precisely what he had been dreading since yesterday, when he had encountered Dewey at the scene of the accident. Crime. Scene of the crime.

"Bookie, I know you don't really dislike me, so you might at least say good morning to me." She settled herself pertly in the visitor's chair and looked at him with a humorous ferocity in her eyes. She knew from experience that she could wear him down, but it always took some doing.

"Good morning," he said with exaggerated cordiality. "Top of the mornin', Mrs. James. And what brings you here?"

"You know perfectly well why I am here. Don't play games with me. Bookie, I want you to know that George and I think this may have been a case of murder."

"Well, Dewey"—Booker permitted himself a smile—"I don't see any reason to hold out on you there. You and George are absolutely correct."

"We are?"

"You are. No reason to keep it a secret. The way this town works, it will be common knowledge by noon."

"Do you want to tell me about it?"

Booker glowered at her. He most certainly did not want to tell her about it; on the other hand, he would have to have all those witnesses back in here this morning, to ask them about anything that they had seen or heard coming from the woods. By afternoon everyone in town would have the general idea. The gun Fielding Booker would keep under wraps, at least until the forensics boys had had a chance with it. But there was no reason not to give Dewey the bare bones of the situation. Perhaps, if he did so, she would leave him in peace.

"Let's just say, Dewey, that the facts in the case point that way. All right? And we, the police of this town, are aware of those facts. We are proceeding apace with our investigation. When the criminal is brought to light, you will be the first to know it, I promise.''

Booker spoke this last sentence without a trace of irony. In fact it was more than likely that Dewey *would* be the first to know. She would probably know before Fielding Booker, at any rate, if her previous experiences as a discreet sleuth could be used as a yardstick.

''Bookie, I have had an idea.'' She looked at him brightly.

''What?'' His eyes widened in mock surprise.

''Please, Bookie. Do be serious. I have had an idea, and I wanted to sound you out on it.''

''That's mighty kind.'' Resignation was creeping into Booker's voice. Dewey plunged ahead.

''Of course, I could do a little digging on my own, but I thought you might take it the wrong way, don't you know. So I felt it would be best if I told you my plans, before going right ahead.''

''I do appreciate that, Dewey,'' said Booker grimly. ''I do indeed.''

''Well, then,'' she went on, taking what she could get, ''I think you ought to do a little looking into that man's background.''

''Background. Such as?''

''Date and place of birth, for starters. Everyone seems so vague about his past. All we know is what he told us— 'California.' It's just so murky, you know.''

''Driver's license said he was twenty-four years of age. Residence was given as Oak Street, in Gorman's Wood.''

''Well, the driver's license would say something, wouldn't it? But, honestly, Bookie, I think if you'll contact the local authorities in the Powells' hometown, we might discover something of interest.''

''Thank you for that, Dewey. As it happens, Emmanuel Slinque is in charge of the funeral arrangements.'' Slinque was a local mortician, a red-haired, lanky giant of a man whom Dewey personally found deeply frightening. She gave a little shiver as Booker continued. ''Cedric Hastings says he would like the boy to be buried with his parents in California, and

Slinque is proceeding to contact the appropriate authorities there.''

"Oh! I see. Well, then." She seemed to reach a decision. "I'll be off, then. But you will tell me, won't you, if you turn up anything interesting?"

Booker smiled broadly—he had won the battle this morning, by a preemptive strike that had knocked the wind right out of Dewey's sails. "You'll find out, one way or another," said Booker amiably, escorting her to the door. "On that you may rely."

16

FIELDING BOOKER DONNED his old felt homburg and headed for Owen Bennet's apartment on Slingluff Avenue. Booker had a feeling about this case. It had all the earmarks of a hastily thought-out crime—and Owen Bennet, Booker felt sure, was his man. Bruce Ward, the guide at the Marshy Point, had seen Bennet buying a box of double-buck just two weeks ago. Now, *that* was evidence.

Bennet had evidently taken advantage of a situation to clear his rival out of the way. He couldn't be sure, even now, that a rivalry such as had existed between the two men would stand up in court as a reason for murder; but Booker had known Owen Bennet for many years. The man was a hothead and a drunk; taken in combination, these forces of his personality might have been enough to loosen the last bolts of his self-restraint.

Booker had little use for Owen Bennet; he disapproved strongly of men who went around town stirring the happy pot of domesticity that prevailed in Hamilton (for Bennet's career as a heartbreaker and a home-wrecker was the stuff of local legend). What was more, Booker had learned through the invaluable Hamilton grapevine that Powell seemed to have set his sights for Maggie Merrit, the soprano soloist. The woman was a good deal older than Powell, but Booker (who considered himself a man of the world in such matters) didn't think the difference in their ages would stop Powell. Not if the attraction was strong enough. Perhaps Maggie had finally given the boot to Bennet in order to take up with the handsome young stranger.

With all these interesting details occupying his mind, Fielding Booker was unprepared for the reception he got from Bennet. The man was cold and supercilious; but there was nothing in his manner to suggest subterfuge.

"Won't you take a little refreshment, Captain?" asked Bennet with exaggerated politeness, when Fielding Booker was seated in his living room.

"No, thank you." Booker looked around. The place wasn't bad, for a bachelor's apartment. He wondered briefly how many of Bennet's women had helped with the decorating scheme—the floral print curtains that matched the sofa certainly bore witness to a woman's touch. Framed portraits of some of the great composers adorned the walls. On one side of the large room was an upright piano, its top piled high with scores. In a corner stood an enormous array of stereo equipment, all very modern and up-to-date; next to the stereo were ranks and rows of LPs, cassette tapes, and compact discs. The man certainly had plenty of money to spend on his record collection, reflected Booker acidly. He considered this conspicuous consumption.

Owen Bennet took a seat in an armchair. Despite the years of drinking and fast living, Bennet was still a remarkably handsome man, athletic and well preserved, with a powerful boyish charm that had swayed many Hamilton ladies. Bennet tossed back a lock of his thick, graying hair and looked at Booker expectantly. "Well?"

"Bennet, I won't insult your intelligence by pretending that this is a social call. I have come to see you on a matter of police business, and I am certain you can guess the nature of it. Now. Suppose you respond in kind, and tell me what you were doing on Saturday afternoon."

"Suppose I don't?" responded Bennet easily.

"Come now, man. There's been murder done. One way or another, you know, we're going to get to the bottom of this affair. It will go easier with you if you cooperate."

"You sound like someone on television, Captain. Where I was and what I was doing is nobody's business but my own."

"You may need an alibi, sir," said Booker firmly.

"An alibi? For the moment when that offensive young pup

took his leave of us? You astonish me, Captain, you honestly do. Believe me," he said, "if I had wished to rid the world of that odious, atonal idiot, I would have done it without calling attention to myself."

"Is that so?"

"That is so." Bennet leaned back comfortably in his chair. "If you wish me to make any kind of a statement, I will have to call Tony Zimmerman. No good trying to make me talk without representation of counsel, you know. I am familiar with the rules."

"I haven't asked for any statement, Bennet. But I would appreciate a little cooperation. If you will simply tell me where you were, and what you were doing, I won't need to bother you again." Booker reflected grimly that this was untrue. Either the man had an alibi or he didn't; but Booker was not one to put faith in alibis. They could easily be concocted and were therefore, *ipso facto*, suspicious. Or so the great detectives of fiction often reasoned; and Booker was inclined to agree.

Owen Bennet stubbornly refused, however, to provide any grist for Booker's mill. Booker took this as a sign that he was on the right track; an innocent man surely would not arouse the suspicions of the police by stonewalling, in so clumsy and irritating a fashion, the dutiful inquiries of Fielding Booker.

"Bennet, a man is dead. And his death was clearly not an accident. It's only fair to tell you that I have heard all about the dustup the other night at the Seven Locks Tavern. Now—I'd like to know the reason behind your antagonism toward him."

"I loathed him on principle. Principally." Bennet looked mildly at Booker. "I loathed him for being an *arriviste* and for singing so badly and so often."

"Come now, sir—" Booker began.

"Captain Booker, I believe I am right in saying that you are not a musician?"

"A musician? No."

"But even so, you may have some sympathy with my feelings. The man had a voice—I'll grant you, he had natural talent. But he was untrained and undisciplined; the merest show-off. His interpretation of the Mozart was enough to make my flesh crawl. Believe me, Captain, that this was reason enough for me to despise him."

"There wasn't some more—er—personal aspect to your quarrel?"

"Good God! I'm a musician, sir. There is nothing more personal, to me, than my Art."

Booker was tempted to roll his eyes, but he restrained the impulse. Why on earth did such oddballs find their way to Hamilton? Life would be much simpler if all the artists would just go away to New York or somewhere and leave them all in peace.

He uttered a low growl. "And what of your relations with Maggie Merrit?"

"Now, that is really none of your business. If you were any kind of a gentleman, you'd know better than to ask such a question."

And so the interview continued. Booker was at last forced to give up; and although he had found the interview exasperating, he departed with a sense of having laid important groundwork for the case he was building.

"Should you care to come forward at any time, Bennet," he said as he took his leave, "I will consider it an act of voluntary cooperation on your part."

"Will you, now? Write me down your good lists, like old Abou Ben Adhem, Captain? That's mighty kind." And with a laugh Owen Bennet closed the door on him.

Alas, Fielding Booker's sensation of progress was destined to be short-lived. Before another day had passed, he would have bad news from Emmanuel Slinque, Mortician.

Slinque, true to his word, had contacted the authorities in Gorman's Wood, California; and the response that came back from the deputy mayor of that good town sent Booker reeling.

"Ah, Slinque," said Booker as the mortician appeared at the police station on Monday morning. "Everything in order? We shall have to hold the body a bit longer than we anticipated, I'm afraid. I needn't go into details just yet, but I'm not certain when we can release it. Will that be a problem?"

Slinque, his carrot-colored hair standing up on end, lowered himself by fits and starts into the visitor's chair. The mortician was so lanky that he looked now like some macabre too-tall crane, folding itself onto its nest. His face, which was ordinarily pale as ashes, was today even more bloodless than usual.

He smiled nervously, showing large yellow teeth between thick, pale lips.

"I am come in person to report," he said in his chronically roundabout style of speaking, "for fear that I should have difficulty making myself understood over the wire."

Booker couldn't abide Emmanuel Slinque. He checked his irritation as far as was possible, however, merely permitting himself a low growl. "Out with it, man."

"The—er, person. Ahem. The person who is at present resting within my establishment is not, I am afraid, the person in question."

"Come again?" Booker sat up, alarmed.

Slinque cleared his throat. "Er, that is to say, the deputy mayor of Gorman's Wood, a man by the name of Rufus Large, spoke to me this morning, over the telephone." He made it sound like an accomplishment; which, given Slinque's style of speech, perhaps it was.

"Yes?"

"It would appear that we have on our hands a pretender to the name of Harrison Powell."

"What?!" Booker thundered. "You mean this corpse—" His face grew purple. "This man is not Harrison Powell?"

"It would appear not. The deputy mayor is well acquainted with the Powell family—or was, until the unhappy demise of the Reverend Powell last year. Harrison Powell, the real Harrison Powell, was arrested six months ago on a charge of dealing in illicit drugs. He is at present serving a sentence of four years in a federal penitentiary."

"Good God almighty." Booker leaned his head on his hands. Why, oh, why, did such things always befall him? He sat up with a start. Was it possible that Dewey's "idea" had been right on the mark? Booker groaned aloud as Emmanuel Slinque went on.

"The deputy mayor was good enough to take down a description of the man we have here. I thought it might be best, taking one thing with another, to ask him to contact your office directly, should any further developments arise. I trust that was satisfactory?"

"Yes, yes. Did the man know who this fellow here might be?"

"The deputy mayor was reluctant to speculate. He assured

me, however, that he would do his utmost to deliver to you a finding, within a day or two."

"A finding." Booker leaned back in his chair and rubbed his palms over his tired eyes. If this man who had been murdered was not Harrison Powell, the whole case was turned topsy-turvy. It was better than even odds that the man was a criminal—at the very least, he had perpetrated criminal fraud here in Hamilton. Perhaps he had been hiding from some of his confederates in crime. But that would mean that the field of suspects would have to be widened to include the whole bloody world, thought Booker sourly.

He roused himself far enough to thank Slinque for his efforts and send him away. Then he sat down heavily in his chair, and, with a reluctance bordering on abhorrence, he reached for the telephone. He wanted to ask George Farnham's advice, but he knew full well that Farnham would be off like a shot to deliver the news to Dewey James. Any hope of a quiet and reasonably rapid unraveling of the crime would be lost in a morass of public opinion and outright interference.

Being a man of honorable dedication to his job, however, Fielding Booker at last picked up the receiver and dialed.

"Well, well," said George Farnham in amazement when he had heard the story. "Well, well."

"George, stop saying, 'well, well,' and give me some advice, man."

"Gladly," said George. He took a bite of a large powdery doughnut—his usual Monday-morning breakfast—and spoke again. "Just tell me what you need."

"For starters," said Booker, "someone is going to have to talk to Cedric Hastings."

"Yes, indeed. Too bad about the sale, I suppose."

"What's that?"

"The sale of the house. It won't be valid now, I'm afraid."

"That's hardly the subject of main importance."

"I suppose not," George admitted, "but it will mean an end to Cedric's pet project. For now, anyway. Cedric's had quite a week, eh? First the burglary at the church and now this."

Fielding Booker had forgotten all about the break-in at the Good Shepherd. He dismissed it from his mind now. The Hamilton police had bigger fish to fry.

"If you wouldn't mind, George, just letting them know. That

would be a start. And I'll need some advice from you about the best way to proceed with this man we have here. Can you do a little research for me on the legal aspects of the thing? I don't want to involve the town in any kind of lawsuit.'' That would be the living end, thought Booker. Things were shaping up to a fine pitch of humiliation as they were.

"Certainly, Bookie. But listen.'' George Farnham couldn't recall ever hearing such distress in Fielding Booker's voice. "It will be all right. And for now, you know, old what's-his-name is perfectly safe with Emmanuel Slinque.''

"Yes. Yes, I suppose he is, if he can abide the confounded conversation.'' Booker rang off.

George Farnham let out a whoop of laughter. Then he grabbed his coat, trotted out the door, and sped to the library. Wait till Dewey heard this one!

Dewey James, however, was not at the library when George Farnham arrived. He had forgotten that Tom Campbell, Dewey's replacement as senior librarian, returned today from his vacation in the Côte d'Azur. George groaned inwardly as Campbell, looking tanned and well rested, stuck out a hand to shake.

"*Bonjour*,'' said Tom grandly. His trip had given him the chance to work on his French, which had grown sadly rusty in Hamilton. Or so he was fond of saying.

"Good to see you back, Tom,'' replied George politely. "Tell me—have you got any idea where Dewey might be?''

"Mrs. James mentioned that she wished to pay a few calls this morning, round about the town. I must say she held down the fort rather nicely in my absence.'' He looked about him with an unwarranted proprietary air. Dewey James had lovingly, and almost single-handedly, administered this fine little library for thirty years. Tom Campbell was a johnny-come-lately who dared to condescend to her about her taste in books and her knowledge of library science. Out here in Hamilton, however, librarians were hard to come by; when she had scaled back her duties at work, Dewey had been forced to take what she could get.

"Yes, indeed,'' replied George, choking back the retort that was forming itself upon his lips. "Well, then. Would you mind just asking her to come round to my office, if she should turn up?''

''Glad to oblige, glad to oblige. *De rien*, as they say.''

Farnham departed and climbed in his car. He had hoped to bring Dewey along with him when he went to call on Cedric Hastings; for George, who was not a member of the church, often felt an unexplained diffidence in the presence of the clergy—even in the presence of Cedric, whom George had known all his life. George sometimes had the uneasy feeling that rabbis and priests and ministers knew something he didn't know—and could never know, in his utterly rational and lawyerly mind.

There was nothing to be done for it, however, so he steeled himself to the task and headed for the rectory.

Back at the police station Fielding Booker was filling in his sergeant on the news.

''This may be bad for us, Mikey,'' he said in a kind voice. ''It could mean that our investigation will have to go statewide. Even nationwide. May have to call in the feds.''

Fenton knew that such a step would be a blow to his captain. The loyal sergeant did his best to pick up his superior's sagging spirits.

''We still haven't heard from the ballistics experts, sir.''

''No, we haven't,'' agreed Booker, who had forgotten the shotgun in the heat of the moment. ''We have not.'' He straightened himself in his chair and made a hasty note. ''Get on to the state lab boys right away, Mike. I want to know where that gun was made and who owns it. I don't care if you have to call every federal and local firearms official in the blasted country. I want to know where it came from and what it was doing there.'' Fielding Booker was feeling better. The gun! There was still a chance that he could track down the murderer through the weapon—even if he hadn't a blessed clue about the victim.

Fenton, feeling that he had accomplished at least one difficult task, headed out to the large communal office where he and the rookie officers had their desks. He leaned over Kate Shoemaker's desk and gave her the news, and the lively young woman sprang to action. Kate Shoemaker, like Fenton, was fond of her captain; this time around she very much wanted him to succeed in putting the cuffs on the murderer. Without any help from their friends.

17

FIELDING BOOKER WAS feeling much better. He put down the telephone and smiled in satisfaction. This business was going to clear up right away.

He was momentarily sorry that he had dispatched George Farnham on that errand to the rectory; it looked, now, as though any question of Hamilton involvement in the matter was unlikely. True, the man had died right here at the Marshy Point; but Booker was becoming swiftly convinced that the roots of the misdeed did not, after all, lie in Hamilton.

He was gratified by the report given him by Rufus Large, the deputy mayor of Gorman's Wood, California. According to Large, Powell had a confederate in his drug dealing: a con artist and ne'er-do-well by the name of Clyde "the Glide" Scobey. Powell and Scobey had been lifelong friends; they had been at school together, sung in the church choir together, and above all, they had been boyhood fellows in delinquency. Shortly after Powell had been put away, Scobey had left Gorman's Wood for parts unknown.

Clyde Scobey had a heavy record of fraud and criminal activity in the little California town; and the deputy mayor's description of the man tallied in every particular with the appearance of the corpse. It was now simply a question of forwarding fingerprints and a dentist's report to California for confirmation.

"Machen!" shouted Booker, finishing up his notes.

Josh Machen appeared in the doorway. "Sir?"

"Machen, get on to the federal boys, will you?" He gave him the details of the report from Gorman's Wood. "I want a full rap sheet on this Scobey character—names, places, dates, known associates."

"Yes, sir."

"Call the U.S. Attorney in Leesburg—what's his name? Dixon. Get Nate Dixon on the phone, pronto."

"Right away, sir," said Machen. He started for the hall, but his superior's voice recalled him to the office.

"Machen. Just a minute."

Machen suppressed a sigh. He knew when his captain was on a roll; these little lectures could take all day. Sometimes they cut right into his lunch hour.

"I want you to look sharp," said Booker, his voice filled with the emotion appropriate to an officer giving commands. "And be quick about it, son. I don't know who Scobey's enemies were, but you can bet he left a trail of them. The fellow was a con man, my boy. Called himself 'the Glide' because he was so slick."

"Yes, sir. I understand, sir."

"I don't need to tell you that con men sometimes get what they ask for."

"No, sir."

"Bad business, this. But at least we can be pretty sure it has nothing to do with us. According to that man Large in California, this Scobey was bad through and through." He picked up his notepad and squinted at it. "When he was fourteen, he was up on a juvenile charge. Tried to extort money from his own grandmother." Booker shook his head heavily and glared at the young rookie.

"Sir." Machen nodded.

"Fellow like that's bound to get himself shot, wouldn't you say?" Having thus delivered himself of his sermon, Booker leaned back in his chair and put his arms comfortably behind his head. He took great comfort in the slow but steady processes of the law. They would get their man. Thank heaven, there would be nothing about this business that could interest any of the well-meaning busybodies in Hamilton. Nobody in Hamilton had even known who the fellow was. The captain smiled benevolently on his young officer. "Well, then—don't stand there. Off with you."

"Yes, sir." Machen departed, sighing with relief.

Thus it was that Fielding Booker, still basking in the glory of a job well done, managed a smile for Dewey James when she appeared, a few moments later, at his officer door.

"Dewey. Come in, come in," said the good captain, rising. "Have a seat. Now. What can I do for you?"

Dewey wasn't fooled by Booker's hearty manner; she knew precisely what it signified. It meant that Booker was, in all likelihood, barking up the wrong tree, and so sure of himself that he wouldn't pay heed unless she was very persistent. She smiled back at him, warming to their little game.

"Bookie. Well—now, you know I wouldn't trespass upon your valuable time if it weren't *absolutely* necessary." She looked at him brightly, and he responded with gallantry.

"Not at all, Dewey, not at all. I rather like having you come round for these little chats." Dewey looked at him warily. When Booker was expansive with her, she knew he was up to something. She attended to him closely as he went on.

"In the old days we used to see so much more of you around here. And of course you are very welcome, whenever we can spare the time from our duties for a little chat. So. Tell me— you have discovered something?"

"No, Bookie. Please don't make fun of me. I just came round to share with you my uneasiness."

"Mighty thoughtful of you, Dewey."

"I don't pretend to thoughtfulness, Bookie. But there is something more going on here than meets the eye."

Booker had to agree with her; but for once he was several steps ahead. He would tell her, of course, the startling news about the corpse. Since George Farnham knew already, there would be no keeping it from Dewey. But Booker would take his time. He was enjoying these moments of success.

"You see," Dewey went on, "I was curious. I don't really know why—except that something about the whole affair had made me nervous right from the start. Hollowness and treachery, you know, follow us disquietly to our graves. And then the little Miles girl was so upset when she saw that picture of General Barker." Booker looked at Dewey with mounting alarm. Was it possible that this dotty old creature had begun to lose her marbles altogether? Booker sincerely hoped not. It was difficult enough to keep her out of his hair when she was in control of her faculties.

"Bookie," said Dewey finally, "have you thought about the house?"

"The house, Dewey?" Booker was mystified but comfortable. For once he held all the cards. He leaned forward and fairly grinned at her. "What house?"

"Cedric's place. Which he sold to Harrison Powell."

"Ah, yes." Booker had forgotten the real estate deal. The fine fog of self-satisfaction that had enveloped him was fast dissipating. Was it possible that there was an angle he had overlooked? He banished the thought.

"Well, of course it would go to that young man's estate. Were there any other Powell children, Bookie?"

Booker looked at her with satisfaction, and a slow smile spread across his handsome features. He adjusted his necktie and leaned toward her, looking solemn.

"What is it, Bookie?"

"I may as well let you know—George knows, and he'll tell you straightaway. In fact, I expected him to have filled you in already." Booker resigned himself to giving her the news. She would suspect him of holding out on her if he didn't—and then, he knew, the battle lines would be drawn. Much better to throw her off the scent right away than to leave her to speculate. When she did, confusion was sure to follow, thought Booker acidly.

He spoke calmly. "The man who died at Marshy Point was not Harrison Powell."

Dewey showed little surprise. She merely sat back in her chair, with a meditative look on her face. "So that was it," she said distractedly.

"That was what?" Booker was annoyed. He hated it when his surprises fell flat.

"I knew there was something wrong about him."

"Come now, Dewey."

"I did, Bookie." She looked at him defiantly. "I told George so, the night of the concert. But he thought I was imagining things."

"Well," said Booker heavily, "it turns out that you were correct."

"Who was he?"

"A crook and a con artist by the name of Clyde Scobey." He sketched out the information, such as it was, for Dewey. "We've got our best people on it right now. Obviously, Scobey was in hiding. He came here—a quiet little town, that he'd heard about from old Dan Powell. He was a family friend, don't forget. So he came here; but somebody tracked him down in spite of his alias. Somebody with a grudge—and a loaded shotgun."

"Dear heaven," said Dewey. "But, Bookie, are you certain?"

"Certain of what?"

"That he was hunted down by some fellow criminal? That seems rather wishful thinking, if you don't mind my pointing it out."

"Now, Dewey," said Booker sternly, feeling the need for authority. "Don't you go thinking about this. It's just a matter of straight police work." Booker's sense of well being, however, was gone. Dewey James always had this effect on him.

He glanced at Dewey, who was deep in thought. His greatest fear was that she would muddle his investigation with some harebrained idea of her own. He moved to put her off the scent.

"Dewey, please. Promise me you will stay out of this investigation."

"Goodness, Bookie. Of course," she said inattentively. "Do you know, I was always suspicious of that boy."

"So you have said. Care to fill me in on the reason of your suspicions? Or is it a secret?"

"Oh, Bookie—there isn't any secret. I simply thought that the young man must have something up his sleeve—something that he wanted. An agenda, if you follow me."

Booker nodded. "But you said nothing?"

"Well, what on earth could I say? Cedric and Charlotte seemed utterly taken with him—Cedric did, at least," she amended, recalling her conversation with Charlotte at Josie's Place. "And his father was Cedric's friend. But I did wonder about him. Good gracious—just think of it! He turned up here out of nowhere and attached himself, like some kind of giant coral or leech or something, to our town. To the church, and to Cedric Hastings. He even took George Farnham hunting."

"Nothing suspicious about that, Dewey. Seemed perfectly

natural, under the circumstances. When we thought he was Harrison Powell.''

Dewey shook her head firmly. ''I don't agree, Bookie. Cedric is a dear—no question about it—but I ask you! Doesn't it seem odd that a man in the full flush of youth, so to speak, should content himself with a quiet, churchy life in our little town?''

''That's it? That's what bothered you?''

''Yes.'' She looked at him with amusement. ''Isn't it enough?''

''I don't suppose you have any idea about why he came here?'' Booker was testing her now. If she was clairvoyant, let her show off her powers.

Dewey rose to the bait. ''Well—now, I'm just guessing, but it would appear to me that he came here with a plan in his head. He asked for Cedric, right away, you know. I picked him up at the bus stop, that first day in town, and gave him a lift straight to the rectory.''

''Ah,'' said Booker. ''He asked for Cedric by name?''

''Not at first. Just asked the way to the rectory. Then we got to talking, because I was curious. Naturally.''

''Naturally.''

''He seemed to know something about Cedric. But he didn't know about his marriage to Charlotte. Which is odd, when you come to think of it. They have been married a full two years, after all; and Dan Powell has only been dead for a year, or even less.''

''That's a good point.'' Booker mulled this one over. He had to hand it to Dewey; she had a way of noticing things. As a rule, this habit of hers made Booker uneasy, for it usually betokened the onset of interference from her. Today, however, he was prepared to listen with an appearance of interest. In short order they would have a list of suspects—names culled from the dregs of Clyde Scobey's wicked past—and they would begin the tedious job of tracing his enemies. Fortunately, Scobey hadn't had time to make many enemies in Hamilton.

Or had he? Booker sat up with a start.

''Great Scott! Owen Bennet!''

Dewey looked at him mildly. ''Come, now, Bookie.''

''Got to be,'' said Booker fiercely. ''Bennet had a motive, all right. And, by gum, he had the right kind of shells.''

"Heavens, Bookie. Everyone knows they argued. But you don't seriously think that their falling out was more than professional jealousy on Bennet's part?"

"Do you think so, Dewey?" rumbled Booker in his best tones of condescending authority. "I suppose it would appear that way to you. Or to any layman. But I'll tell you, this crime has all the earmarks of violent dislike. It was clearly thought out well in advance. And everyone in town knows that Bennet is a rare marksman. I'm afraid," he said, rising and pulling on a hefty tweed jacket, "that I will have to get to the bottom of this little affair between the two men."

"But, Bookie—"

"Now, Dewey," said Booker firmly. "I appreciate your interest." He took her by the arm and fairly pulled her up out of the chair. "I'm afraid I must pop around to see Cedric. Then I plan to pay a call on Owen Bennet. Promise me, Dewey, that you will not obstruct me in the course of discharging my duties."

"Yes, indeed," she replied, feeling deeply unhappy. There was something more going on here, she knew. She did not doubt the sincerity of Booker's interest in Owen Bennet; but she doubted that the displaced tenor had been sober long enough to hatch a plan of murder. There were other people, however, whose marksmanship had not been thus dulled. There were other people in town with plenty of ammunition.

Feeling unsettled, but with an idea in her head, Dewey took her leave.

18

GEORGE FARNHAM HAD paid his call at the rectory, telling a stunned and shaken Cedric Hastings about the strange man who was now resting eternally in a holding pattern at Emmanuel Slinque's funeral home. As George departed, Fielding Booker arrived, a new look of worry and determination on his broad, handsome face.

"Cedric," said Booker, taking a seat with the reverend in the den. "I'm afraid I must talk to you about this business. George has filled you in, at my request, about who the dead man was. Or perhaps I should say," Booker went on uncertainly, "about who he is not."

Cedric Hastings nodded but made no reply. Booker went on gently.

"Cedric, did you have no idea that this man wasn't Harrison Powell?"

Cedric shook his head slowly. His cheeks were flushed, and his eyes glinted strangely behind his wire-rimmed spectacles. He ran a finger idly around the inside of his clerical collar and seemed to have trouble getting his breath.

At last he spoke. "No idea, Bookie." He leaned his arms upon his knees and gave the rug on the floor a brief, sour glance. Then he returned his gaze to the policeman, and his customary noncommittal air returned as he spoke. His voice was clear, and he had regained his perfect mastery of elocution.

"I am utterly flabbergasted; and rather dismayed, as well, I don't mind saying. After all, we considered him one of us—one of the family.'' He leaned back in his chair and gazed reflectively at a large fish tank on a table in the corner. The tank was beautifully maintained, Booker noted, and the inhabitants seemed to swim about with rather more vitality than was customary with captive fish. Booker wondered idly whose idea the fish had been—Charlotte's or Cedric's?

The reverend took in a deep breath and spoke once more. ''Still and all, Bookie, I can't say I'm sorry we knew the boy. Whoever he was. He did a great deal for the church, you know. We can't take that away from him.''

''No.'' Booker shifted uneasily in his chair and looked about him. The walls were lined from floor to ceiling with books; more books peeked out of corners and spilled over the surface of every table and windowsill in the room. There were dozens of Bibles, in all shapes and sizes, and these were flanked by missals, prayer books, and hymnals. On a high shelf was a long row of books with titles in Latin; and below it some uninviting tomes with Greek characters on the spine.

Fielding Booker found himself momentarily discomfited by the sober-looking volumes; like many people, he was slightly unnerved by such frank evidence of faith. But his mind was greatly relieved when he noticed, next to the old green leather sofa, a rank of about three dozen paperbacks—all nearly identical and reassuringly familiar. There could be no mistake: The Reverend Cedric Hastings had collected the adventures of Perry Mason, that excellent attorney-at-law! Booker was himself a Gardner fan, and he applauded the reverend's choice in fiction. Well, now, thought Booker. What we have here is the Case of the Trumped-Up Tenor.

''Have the police any idea of his identity?'' Cedric asked at last.

Booker nodded. ''He was at least a friend of the family—of the Powell boy, that is. We are waiting for details from the police in California, but I am inclined to believe that he is a known criminal by the name of Clyde Scobey. He and Harrison Powell had been lifelong friends, apparently—which would explain why he knew about you.''

Hastings nodded. ''Yes, indeed it would.'' His eyes sparkled. ''If it weren't so distressing, you know, I might find the situation rather fascinating. I don't recall in my lifetime having been the target of criminal activity. I wonder if I can turn it to advantage somehow.''

"Er, yes," replied Booker, wondering what on earth the rector meant. "Put it in a sermon or something."

"Precisely," agreed Hastings. "I wonder if that wouldn't work." He went to his desk and made a quick note, looking up at Booker with a little birdlike nod. "Good idea. Thank you, Bookie.''

Booker began to feel more at ease, and he set about questioning Cedric. There was not much, however, that the cleric could tell him. He had never, until two months ago, laid eyes on his friend Daniel's son; but he hadn't for a moment been suspicious.

"I don't understand," said Booker, "how he managed to pull it off. He must have known a great deal about you, to make you both believe his impersonation. But to keep it up?"

Cedric Hastings considered the point. "He didn't, really, you know. He didn't know much about us at all," he said finally, with a shake of his head. "But then, that didn't surprise me. Dan and I were close, but our friendship was an intellectual one. We wrote to each other, back and forth, about ideas and philosophies. He didn't share with me the details of his personal life—except, of course, to tell me, many years ago, that Lucy had died.''

"You knew he had a son?"

"Oh, yes, I knew there was a son," said Cedric slowly. "That much I knew. And I was prepared to believe that this young man was he.''

Just then the back door opened, and Charlotte and Ben made a noisy arrival in the hall. Charlotte, her face flushed from the cold, fresh air, poked her head in the den.

"Captain?" She looked swiftly at her husband.

"Hello, Mrs. Hastings," said Booker, rising.

"Darling, we've had some rather startling news, I'm afraid."

"Is everything all right?"

"Sit down, and we'll tell you about it, ma'am," replied Booker. Charlotte did as he bade her, divesting a squirming Ben of his outergarments and maintaining her poise. "Hold still, sweetheart," she told the boy.

Booker explained the situation, watching Charlotte's reaction with interest. She seemed somehow more worried than angry.

"If you don't mind," said Booker, "I'm afraid I'll have to ask you a few questions."

"All right," Charlotte replied calmly with a searching glance for her husband. "Just let me take Ben up, if you don't mind." She departed and returned a few moments later, taking a seat in an old rocking chair near a window. She shook back her curls and looked stolidly at Booker.

"Captain Booker, if that man was really someone called Clyde Scobey, why did he come looking for us?"

"That's what we intend to discover, ma'am. It appears he was a friend of the Powell family, but I'm afraid he was bad through and through. He seems to have been some in trouble with the law; and it rather looks as though the rectory was simply a convenient hiding place for him."

Charlotte let out a low, bitter laugh. "He took us in. That's for sure. I thought he really cared for Ben."

"Hush, my dear," said Cedric soothingly. "Do you know, I think you are right about that. He cared for Ben and he cared for us—the church, that is."

"Well, suppose you just tell us who he was? And why he came here to get himself killed at the Marshy Point Ducking Club?" She began to weep very softly.

Booker cleared his throat. "I apologize for intruding at such a difficult time, Mrs. Hastings. I knew this must be extremely upsetting for you both. But if the police are to get to the bottom of this mystery, I shall have to pursue rather unpleasant lines of inquiry. I may, in fact, have to hit rather close to home. I'm sure you understand."

Charlotte had composed herself while Booker was making his speech, and now she nodded, looking at him with clear, honest eyes.

"Go ahead, Captain."

"Thank you, ma'am. I should like to know, for starters, what your feelings were toward this young man."

"Now, just wait a minute," said Cedric Hastings, his cheeks draining of color. "What are you getting at, Bookie?"

"Take it easy, Cedric. Please." Booker shifted his glance to Charlotte. "You and your husband befriended him; you took him into your lives. Now. I take it that you, like your husband, had no clue that he was not who he said he was."

Charlotte shook her head slowly. "No clue. What a silly thing to do," she said slowly, with a worried look toward her husband. "Why on earth, Cedric?"

The Reverend Hastings stared at her. There was an urgency in his eyes that even Fielding Booker could not fail to spot.

"Did the fellow substantiate himself in any way?"

"Yes," Charlotte replied firmly. "He knew all about Cedric, about Cedric and Dan's adventures in Kerangani. Well, of course he would. He himself said that Dan used to talk about it all the time."

"And on the basis of that you took him into this house?"

"There was no reason not to, Bookie," Cedric Hastings pointed out. "We had no reason to disbelieve him. After all, he was the proper age and had the right sort of way about him, if you know what I mean. And then there was the choir, and the way he helped Julia Boucher with the bookkeeping—it was, if you don't mind my pointing it out, rather an elaborate impersonation. One would have to have a very suspicious mind indeed to think that there was some dark purpose to it."

Charlotte laughed suddenly. "It must have been awfully boring for him. Here he was, masterminding a clever ruse—and suddenly he found himself going to church all the time, and singing the tenor solo in the Mozart *Requiem*. Hardly fast living. I wonder that he bothered."

"So do I, come to think of it," replied Booker. He turned to Cedric. "Well, then. Suppose you tell me all about Owen Bennet."

Charlotte looked up sharply, wariness in her eyes.

Hastings glanced at Booker. "If we're going to discuss my parishioners, Bookie, I'd just as soon preserve the norms," he explained. "Confidentiality between priest and penitent, and all that."

"Yes, of course," replied Booker, feeling tremendously ill-at-ease.

"Darling, would you mind?" Cedric asked his wife.

"Of—of course not, dear."

Looking shaken, Charlotte rose slowly from her seat and headed out of the little room. She pulled the door fast closed behind her and went to the kitchen to fix herself a cup of tea.

The bird Pindar, looking rattier than ever, shrieked as she entered. "*Thanatos!*" cried the bird. "*Thanatos!*"

"Quiet, you stupid bird," said Charlotte.

Charlotte Hastings had little Latin and less Greek; but she knew the meaning of this word, at least. The bird uttered it all day long.

Thanatos.

Death.

19

WHILE THE VALIANT forces of the Hamilton constabulary were thus pursuing the trail of wrongdoers, Dewey James was on a fishing expedition. She didn't cast her net in the roaring rapids of the Boone River; nor did she float a bobber on the placid shallows of Cooper Lake. She fished instead in the murky depths of the land records office, in the dim nether recesses of the Grain Merchants Exchange Building.

The imposing Greek Revival edifice had once been the hub of commerce in Hamilton. In those days Hamilton had bustled; farmers and traders and merchants had come from all corners of the young nation to buy and sell their goods; and the huge granite building had rung with the clamor of their raised voices.

Today, the large stone-walled rooms were quiet. The cavernous main hall was, on occasion, enlivened by a spirited town-council meeting or fete of some sort; but for the most part the diminished civic body that now functioned here had something of the air of a child playing dress-up in clothes that were much too large.

At the end of a warrenlike hall on the first floor, in a musty room that received no daylight, an enormous stack of yellow forms waited to be sorted. And behind the forms, surrounded by the records and the history of the legal proceedings of the town, sat the county clerk: a blue-haired woman of indeterminate age by the name of Hilda Beane.

Dewey had had experience with Hilda Beane. The woman was a waking nightmare of a civil clerk; she had raised to a high art the act of pretending not to notice one. Hilde Beane, in fact, could fairly be described as officious, snappish, and slow. At least, thought Dewey, as she approached the woman's lair, she is not nasty, brutish, and short. Dewey always liked to look on the positive side.

"Just wait right there," snapped Hilda Beane as Dewey made her way to the counter. "I don't have much time today, so you will simply have to wait."

"Thank you, and good morning," said Dewey, managing a polite response to this Looking-Glass logic. She watched in amazement as the woman took an enormous rubber stamp from a swiveling rack and began to pound her way through a thick pile of documents. When she reached the bottom, she looked up, sniffed, and adjusted her eyeglasses, which were shackled to her alabaster person by a shiny length of chain.

"Yes?"

"I've come to look at a deed, if I may," said Dewey firmly.

"Do you know the number?"

"Dear heavens, no," said Dewey. Where on earth did one learn the number? "Perhaps you could tell me."

Hilda Beane withdrew a long, sharp pencil from the nub of blue hair at the back of her neck; with this pencil, she gestured across the room to a large file cabinet made up of hundreds of tiny drawers.

"The properties are recorded in those files, there, sorted geographically. You may look, but don't touch, and do not remove the cards. When you find the name of the selling party, make a note of the number. Then cross-check it with the name of the purchasing party in those binders over there." She gestured again with her pencil, this time to the opposite end of the cavernous room, where an imposing array of ring binders caused their shelves to droop dismayingly. "The number of the deed is recorded in the binders. When you have that number, you may come to see me."

"Thank you very much," said Dewey, shaking back her silvery hair and marching stolidly toward the file cabinet.

The search took comparatively little time. Dewey was stunned by the Gordian complexity of the system, but she found it a fairly easy code to crack. Of course, Dewey's level of confidence was high—she had, after all, been a librarian for thirty years. The county clerk, thought Dewey, would have excelled as a cryptographer, encoding dismal messages to send to forlorn spies in perilous and boring places.

She jotted down the number and returned to the front counter. Then she waited patiently for several minutes while Hilda Beane thumped her way through another towering pile of yellow forms.

"Have you considered putting some of this material on a computer?" Dewey asked at last, unable to control herself.

It was a rash speech, and it misfired badly, prompting Hilda Beane to ignore Dewey for another full five minutes. But finally, when the last piece of paper had been punished by the rubber stamp, Hilda Beane was at last forced to get up from her desk and retrieve Dewey's information.

If anyone had asked Dewey what she was looking for, she wouldn't have had an answer. But that was sometimes the way with fishing expeditions. Dewey thoughtfully studied the deed, which recorded the sale by Cedric Hastings to Harrison Powell of the Hastings family property.

She really had just come to look, propelled by her unsettling curiosity about the transaction. Since the death of Harrison Powell—or rather Clyde Scobey—that curiosity had grown.

But Dewey wasn't prepared for the information that the document provided. "Excuse me," she said to Hilda Beane. The woman looked up sharply. "This number here," said Dewey, unwavering now that she had gone so far, "is this meant to be in thousands?"

"What do you mean, thousands?" Hilda Beane got up to look. She pushed her glasses more firmly down on her nose and squinted. "Thousands? No. That's it, right there."

"One hundred dollars?"

"If it says one hundred dollars, it was one hundred dollars. See?" She pointed. "Certified by the bank and notarized. One hundred dollars."

Dewey thanked Hilda Beane and made her way slowly out through the cavernous hallway of the old building. Cedric Hastings had sold the house to Powell for one hundred dollars? What on earth had that man been up to? Dewey shook her head as she headed out. Her heart sank, and she feared the worst.

She stepped out into the chilly November sunshine and looked at her watch. It was nearly a quarter to eleven. She really ought to go back to the library, but the thought of spending the morning listening to Tom Campbell talk about the Côte d'Azur and spatter his speech with French words was too much for her. She would leave it, for now, and try to tend to a few other errands while she sorted through the implications of the fact she had just learned.

She headed up the street, glancing in at the window of the Tidal Wave Beauty Salon as she passed. Doris Bock had assembled quite a crowd today; but the place always was jammed in the immediate aftermath of a local scandal or crisis. Last week, after the brouhaha at the Fall Concert and the ensuing fistfight at the Seven Locks Tavern, Doris Bock had been obliged to stay open late two nights running. Dewey smiled as she thought about the women of Hamilton who had already spent their hairdressing money for the month of November. They must be kicking themselves. What a golden opportunity they were missing today at the Tidal Wave!

Dewey noted with interest that Beverly Simms was inside, sitting peaceably under the bonnet of a large dryer. Beverly Simms was a local real-estate agent; and everyone in town knew that she had spent a great deal of time and energy in her unsuccessful efforts to unload Cedric's old place. Here was a piece of luck, thought Dewey. Perhaps Doris would be able to fit her in for a quick wash and set.

She swung the door open and was greeted cordially by one and all. Her arrival was serendipity for Doris Bock; the fortunes of her *maison de beauté* depended greatly upon the presence or absence of people who knew something "inside" about local affairs. Dewey James was widely considered to have a hot line to Fielding Booker; she would be sure to have the latest information on the grisly murder at the Marshy Point Ducking Club.

But Dewey, this morning, had come to dig for information, not to give it away. She kept to herself the news Bookie had given her this morning, because she was eager to see if she could learn anything from Beverly Simms. If Dewey told the Tidal Wave patrons that the dead boy was not even Harrison Powell, she would not get far with her little inquiries. So she kept her counsel.

Doris Bock cleared the decks, and Dewey was soon settled in the large red vinyl armchair before the sink.

"Now, Mrs. James," began Doris as she lathered Dewey

energetically, "please tell us what you make of all this non-sense."

Several ladies leaned in closer; Jan Duke, who was having a perm baked under the heat of an ancient hair dryer, went so far as to turn off the roaring machine, the better to hear the proceedings.

Dewey answered evasively. "I don't have an idea, really, Doris. It seems completely random to me. A dreadful accident."

"Accident? Hah!" said Beverly Simms, a smile crossing her broad and cheerful face. "More likely a crime of passion. He *was* murdered, you know. I had dinner with Josie last night, and she had heard Mike Fenton say so."

So the word was out, thought Dewey.

"Mary Barstow liked him," put in Jan Duke, a vivacious blond of thirty-five or so. Her husband, Barry, was Hamilton's premier dealer in rare books; the Dukes were generally considered rather an intellectual pair. "Barry and I saw them together at the movies last week." Mary Barstow, the pert dental hygienist who worked for Dr. Langford, was not one to keep her admiration under wraps.

"Mary Barstow likes every man she meets," pointed out Sarah Mintzer, owner of the Negligée Nest. Sarah's intimate knowledge of Hamilton's changing tastes in lingerie gave her an inside track on the rising and falling fortunes of romance in the little town. Sarah Mintzer, thank goodness, knew how to be discreet. Where Mary Barstow was concerned, however, discretion was beside the point.

"Maybe this time Mary couldn't deal with rejection," offered Beverly Simms.

"Who said anything about rejection?" replied Jan. "They did go to the movies together. Maybe she loved him."

"Somebody didn't like him, that's for sure," said Doris, testing Jan's curls. She was keeping things on track; Doris didn't like the conversation at her establishment to stray too far from the point. "He sure was unpopular with Owen Bennet, for example."

"Sure," said Jan, "but Owen hates everybody. That is, unless he's trying to get to first base with them." There was a gentle murmur of assent from the crowd; Jan had a point. Owen Bennet, for all of his trail of broken hearts in Hamilton, didn't have many friends. "You know what *I* think?" she went on. "I think maybe there was some kind of funny business at the rectory."

"Come off it, Jan," protested Doris, moving to unclip the curls of Beverly Simms. "What on earth do you mean?" The expression on the good proprietress's face, however, gave her away. Dewey remembered uneasily how Doris Bock had watched the tête-à-tête between Charlotte and Powell at Josie's Place. She hoped that Doris had the good sense not to leap to conclusions.

"Charlotte spent a lot of time with him out at that old place, fixing it up," she said.

"Not really?"

"Yes. Really. Michael Kayon, the architect, told me. He came into our bookstore last week. He said that Charlotte Hastings seemed to be taking quite an interest in the restoration."

"Well, now, really, Jan, that's hardly suspicious," replied Dewey, who by now had her head swathed in a towel. "She probably was acting out of loyalty to Cedric. Didn't want Harrison to ruin the place."

"What I'd like to know," put in Sarah Mintzer, "is why he came here in the first place. Why did he even buy that silly old house?"

The ladies looked expectantly at Beverly Simms. The realtor, however, gave no sign that she knew of anything odd about the sale. Of course, thought Dewey, she wouldn't let on—not if she wanted to survive in this town. Still, the amount of the sale price was public knowledge—Dewey had easily found it out. So it did seem rather odd that Beverly didn't offer this tidbit. At the very least such a justification would have dispelled any aura of failure that clung to her own efforts to sell the place.

Clearly, Beverly Simms was not in the know. "I can't imagine why he wanted that place," she said firmly. "The last prospect I showed it to said it would need at least fifty thousand dollars' worth of work before it was livable. The property, of course, is beautiful—that's why old Stewart Mackenzie was interested. But these days people don't just go around buying up property for its looks. Not unless they're millionaires."

"Not even then," put in Dewey with a laugh. "Or they wouldn't be millionaires for long."

"No. Mrs. James is right," agreed Doris Bock vigorously as she pinned up Dewey's locks. "So—why did he want it?"

"Sentimental reasons," suggested Sarah Mintzer. "Because it reminded him of Charlotte."

"How could it remind him of Charlotte?" asked Jan Duke reasonably. "She never even lived there. Old Felix Hastings was the one who lived there."

"Maybe he wanted to steal her away from Cedric," said Beverly Simms, mulling it over. "After all, you know . . ." She left the sentence unfinished. But everyone knew what was on her mind. Harrison Powell had been a very handsome young man.

"No," said Jan Duke at last. "Because if that's what he wanted, it would be much simpler *not* to buy the place. It would be much easier just to run away together. If that's what they wanted."

"Maybe Charlotte didn't want it," offered Dewey simply. She firmly believed that Charlotte Hastings was deeply in love with her husband. She had only, for documentation, the way Charlotte looked in the kitchen—utterly at home. It must be love, Dewey reasoned, for nothing else on earth would persuade a beautiful young woman to tolerate that seedy, squawking old parrot of Cedric's. To Dewey's mind, the fact that the bird still lived provided conclusive evidence of Charlotte's deep and abiding affection for her husband.

Dewey James departed the Tidal Wave relaxed and thoroughly intrigued. It was clear that Cedric Hastings had kept the surprising terms of the sale very dark, indeed; for Beverly Simms was nobody's fool when it came to real estate. It was all exceedingly strange.

Like it or not, Dewey was going to have to fill Bookie in on this vital intelligence. Only Providence knew what he would do with the information when he had grasped it, but she hoped the police captain would think carefully before he reached any conclusion.

In the meantime, Dewey would go home to think these matters through. There was something wrong about the whole picture, but she could not put her finger on it.

20

By the end of the afternoon all of Hamilton was reeling from the shocking revelations about the man who now lay within the cool and unregenerative purview of Emmanuel Slinque, Mortician. Hamilton's good people were dismayed. The dead man had not been Harrison Powell at all, but a criminal from California who had come to hide himself in their midst. Some shook their heads. "Clyde Scobey"—even his name sounded sinister, now that they thought about it. You can run, said others, but you can't hide. It had only been a matter of time until his past caught up with him.

By five-thirty the Seven Locks Tavern was full to bursting point. There, while Nils Reichart kept the beer flowing fast and foamy, people discussed and improved on the news. The clientele of that establishment were, in the main, large men who knew how to handle a gun. When the incident at Marshy Point had first been reported, many had shaken their heads and looked serious. There but for the grace of God, some of them said, go we.

Paradoxically, these sturdy citizens, with their solid outdoor amusements, were somehow comforted by the thought that it had been murder. The hunting season now held less of a threat for hardy providers; Reichart's customers laughed and talked freely, once more, about their plans to bag a goose or a duck. For the ducks, of course, this change of heart was no laughing matter.

The ebullient and speculative mood of the conversation at

the bar was mirrored at the Tidal Wave Beauty Salon, where Doris Bock was again burning the midnight oil to accommodate the influx of custom. Mary Barstow, the dental hygienist, found herself unable to keep away; she was having her third manicure of the week and reveling in the temporary spotlight into which this business had thrust her. She had, after all, gone to the movies with the man.

The other ladies flocked around her, hungry for information; the stranger had always been appealing, but now he was mysterious, even dangerous. And most certainly murdered! Mary Barstow played it to the hilt, answering their questions coyly and doing her best to look as though she knew more than she was telling. Doris Bock's customers played along, although they fully comprehended how impossible it was for Mary Barstow ever to know more than she told.

At the Church of the Good Shepherd, however, the mood was more somber. Cedric Hastings had come by to talk to Julia, who had been shaken, Cedric later told Charlotte; but all in all Julia Boucher seemed to take it well.

Wally Penberry accepted the tidings in stride when Julia Boucher came to the music room in the early evening. Penberry was a good man, but—like most great musicians—single-minded; his chief concern at this moment was to find himself a new tenor for the choir. It was really too bad; for Harrison Powell—or whoever he was—had had a rare gift. It would be difficult to find anyone to fill his shoes.

"How about talking to Owen?" Julia Boucher suggested. Her voice was muffled; she was deep in the large wardrobe where the choir robes were kept, straightening the purple shrouds on their hangers.

Penberry shook his head and laughed gently. "I'm afraid I'd be sent away with a flea in my ear."

"I don't know about that," responded Julia. "He came by here this morning, you know."

"Who did?"

"Owen. He was looking for Cedric—at least, that's what he told me." Julia rubbed her thin, dry hands together softly. "But I had the feeling he had come to make it up to you."

"Well, now," said Penberry, his broad face lighting up. "Do you think he would? Because"—he dived for a pile of papers on the piano and came up with a handwritten sheet of music—"I've just finished this little setting of the Twenty-third Psalm, and I'd like to try it out for the early service on Sunday. But I need a soloist."

Julia smiled to herself. Wally had a one-track mind; but that was all to the good, she felt. The Hamilton Music Society really did them proud. "Shall I call him?"

"That would be magnificent, Julia," said Penberry, beginning to sound out the first few notes of the tenor solo on the piano. Penberry could carry a tune, but his voice was most surprisingly lacking in any quality except absolute accuracy. "The Lord is my shepherd," Penberry sang in his remarkable way. He turned to Julia. "As him if he could get over here this evening, would you?"

Julia Boucher obliged; and that was how Fielding Booker came to arrest a man for the crime of murder.

"Hah!" said Fielding Booker, gloating. "Hah!" He put aside his binoculars and turned to Mike Fenton. "Take a look, my boy. He's going to scoot, you mark my words."

Booker and Fenton were sitting in the front seat of Booker's car, which was parked inconspicuously on Slingluff Avenue, across from a small apartment building. On the second floor they could make out a figure moving quietly about in the lighted apartment. Back and forth the figure moved; even without the binoculars it was easy for Fenton to see that Owen Bennet was packing some kind of suitcase.

Booker was filled with a heightened intensity; he sat utterly still, watching his prey. He shivered comfortably in the darkened car, relishing—with an almost military appreciation—the slight hardship of going without heat for an hour or so. He pulled an ancient cashmere scarf closer about him and rubbed his hands together appreciatively. Now, *this* was police work.

Fenton shifted uneasily. "Sir?"

"Yes?" Booker whispered harshly.

"Uh, sir—what about the gun?"

"What about the gun, Mikey?"

"Kate said she was following up a lead on the owner. Don't you think we should radio her?"

Booker shook his head. "It would call attention to our presence. That can wait. A bird in the hand, my boy. A bird in the hand."

"Yessir." Fenton stifled a yawn and stole a look at his watch. Seven-fifteen. They had been here for forty-five minutes, watching as Owen Bennet arrived home from somewhere—probably the Canalside Tavern, Booker had speculated, since a discreet inquiry had shown that Bennet hadn't been at the Seven Locks. Nils Reichart wouldn't have Bennet on the premises; not after the scene with Powell. Scobey. Whichever.

Fenton was mildly curious about what Bennet was up to; but he was more interested in learning what Kate Shoemaker had to report. He sighed quietly.

The light went out in the window across the street, and in a few moments Owen Bennet emerged. In his hand he carried a curiously shaped brown grip, wide and almost square, about the size and shape of an old-fashioned shell box.

Booker grunted in satisfaction.

Bennet looked left and right, then headed off up Slingluff Avenue toward Howard Street. The policemen watched as he made an unsteady right turn onto Adams Bridge Road; then Booker started the engine.

"Key to this kind of operation, Mikey, is to take it slow and easy."

"Yessir."

"Now, our quarry is on foot—so this should be a piece of cake. Steady as she goes." He put the car in neutral and let it coast gently down to the intersection; then he shifted into gear and followed, still without turning on the headlights, as Bennet made for the river.

"Probably has someone waiting to pick him up," asserted Booker.

"Yessir," agreed Fenton, who was by no means sure of this.

Owen Bennet reached the crest of Adams Bridge and leaned heavily over the rail, watching the swirling water of the river below. In the dull yellow lamplight they could see the hollows beneath his eyes. He looked haggard and defeated.

"Sir?" Fenton felt a nervous rush. "You don't think—"

"Looks like a man with a conscience to me, my boy."

"Shouldn't we do something?"

Booker nodded and pulled the car over. They climbed out silently and made their way stealthily toward Bennet.

Their approach, on the still and quiet little bridge over the river, was not as silent as Booker might have hoped. Before they were within fifty yards, the quarry had spotted them.

''Hoho!'' called Bennet in a taunting voice. ''The Law!'' He hefted the leather case up for them to see. ''Say good-bye!''

''Blast it, Mike! Hustle, boy!'' Booker and Fenton charged, but they were too far away. Bennet gave them a superior smile and tossed the case, with a curiously vicious movement, over the railing and into the rushing water below.

21

WHILE FIELDING BOOKER stood on Adams Bridge, cursing ferociously, Dewey James was thinking. She had spent the early part of the evening tending to chores around the house, feeding Starbuck and Isaiah, and trying to come to some kind of conclusion about what she had learned from Hilda Beane. The situation was rife with complications; and it seemed, to Dewey's experienced and sympathetic mind, to have all the earmarks of a tragedy. By this term she was not comprehending the death of Clyde Scobey; she wasn't sure, now, how she felt about that. But there were many other people to be considered.

"Clyde Scobey, indeed," she remarked to Isaiah, who was finishing his dinner. "Honestly, Isaiah. I think there is something rather pathetic in the whole affair."

His bowl now empty, Isaiah rewarded his mistress with his full attention. Dewey shook her head sadly. "I think Bookie is barking up the wrong tree," she said flatly. "But goodness knows how I'll persuade him of that. I know one thing, however: I must talk to George."

She telephoned Farnham, who was delighted at the prospect of a visit from her; and in less than half an hour she was at the old mill building that he now called home.

"Dewey!" George exclaimed happily as he opened the door. "How about a bite to eat, my dear?"

"Thank you, George, no. I've had my supper, but I just felt I must talk to you."

"Coffee, then."

126

"That would be lovely." She followed him into the kitchen, talking as they went. "George, I have found out something rather perplexing. I have been thinking and thinking about it, trying to make sense of it."

"Yes, indeed," said George, grinning broadly. "Come sit down, and we'll talk." George Farnham was feeling pleased with himself. Dewey must have heard the news about Powell's true identity—and she had turned to him! Not only that, but George was one up on Dewey—Booker had told him first.

They settled themselves at George's kitchen table, and Dewey stared thoughtfully out through the large sliding-glass door to the riverbank. The trees that fronted the river were nearly bare; thick clouds were massing in the west, beyond the fields and hills on the other side of the rushing waters. It promised to be a cold Thanksgiving, Dewey reflected, wishing suddenly that her daughter, Grace, could join her here in Hamilton. Since Brendan's death, she had never shaken the sadness that seemed to absorb her at this time of year.

George, brewing coffee in a sleek Italian coffeepot, roused Dewey from her reverie.

"So you've heard the news about our mysterious stranger," he said with a smile.

"I have," replied Dewey firmly. "And I can't say that I was surprised."

"No?" He was disappointed. The news had certainly taken George Farnham by surprise.

"No." Dewey shook her head. "You will recall that I always said that he was too good to be true."

"So you did, my dear," replied George placatingly. "So you did. Drink up, and tell me—since you knew he was too good to be true—who killed him? And why?"

Dewey shook her head. "I hate to admit it, George, but do you know I'm afraid to think about it?"

"Come now, Dewey. You aren't serious?" There were few things that Dewey James was afraid to confront; George was intrigued.

"Oh, yes, I am," she averred. "Deadly serious."

"But it might have been anyone. Bookie says the man had an extensive criminal record. Extorted money from his own grandmother, or something like that."

"'Sharper than a serpent's tooth,' no doubt. I'm sure Clyde

Scobey was a blackguard,'' Dewey concurred. "But, George—how preposterous, really. Do you honestly think, for even a minute, that some ruthless fellow criminal tracked him down all the way from California to Hamilton—to the Marshy Point Ducking Club, to dispose of him in front of six or seven witnesses?''

"Well, now that you put it that way, my dear—''

"Just so. I knew you would agree with me. Now you will see why I am perplexed—because I have found out something else. And I need your help, George.''

George was only too pleased to be of assistance. From time to time Dewey enjoyed going out on a limb; and he delighted in watching her, and abetting, wherever possible, her more daring feats. He took great pleasure in his role of accomplice, cheering section, and holder of the safety net. In recent years Dewey's goading and prodding and meddling had helped Booker get to the bottom of more than one serious crime in the little town. Through it all, George Farnham had stood by, patient and helpful. He was the best sort of ally—a willing volunteer.

"Whatever you need, Dewey dear, I'm at your service. But you'll have to fill me in first, you know.''

"Yes,'' agreed Dewey with a smile. "Well. I have been to see that dreadful woman, George.''

"Which dreadful woman is that?'' he asked, mildly amused. Hamilton boasted its share of dreadful women to choose from, to be sure.

"Hilda Beane,'' said Dewey with distaste.

"The Blue-haired Dragon?'' George laughed aloud. "You are intrepid, my dear. Whatever took you to see her?''

"I don't quite know what prompted me—idle curiosity, I guess. But here is the thing that troubles me. Cedric sold his house to that man Scobey—''

"Ah, well, not to worry.'' Farnham was momentarily disillusioned; Dewey's perplexity was over nothing more than business. Well, he could settle her mind. "Because the sale was based on a fraudulent representation as to the parties involved,'' he said in lawyerly tones, "the deal will be void. Easy enough for Cedric to handle—and of course I shall offer my assistance, if he needs it.''

"No, no, George,'' Dewey protested. "Honestly—you're so

pleased with yourself for being in Bookie's confidence that you're not even listening to me. What bothered me were the terms.''

"Terms? Of the sale, do you mean?"

She nodded. "He sold the house—to whomever it was he sold it—for a hundred dollars.''

"What?" Farnham sat back in his chair, astounded.

"That's right." Dewey nodded deeply. "I went right in and looked at the records. It was all down in black and white. And I can assure you, George, that I made no mistake. I asked Hilda Beane to verify it for me.''

"Well, I'll be doggone," said Farnham. He shook his head in amazement. "That money was supposed to pay for the Elder Care project. I can't imagine what would prompt Cedric to do such a thing.''

"Can't you, now?" Dewey looked at her friend shrewdly.

"Uh-oh," said George evenly. He put down his coffee cup with a thump. "Are you thinking what I'm thinking?"

"Yes, I'm afraid so," admitted Dewey.

"Well, well.''

"Indeed," said Dewey with a hint of sadness in her voice.

"We ought to tell Bookie.''

"Do you think so?" She stirred her coffee thoughtfully. "He has persuaded himself that Owen Bennet is the culprit.''

"Ah. Good old Bookie.''

"But this information that I have lights the subject from rather a different angle, wouldn't you say?"

"Yes. Yes, I would.''

"How shall we handle this, George?"

Farnham thought. "There is, naturally, the legal side of things to be considered.''

"That's right." George was following her lead beautifully, reflected Dewey.

"Perhaps it would be a good idea for me to have a word with Cedric in the morning.''

"I thought of that. But I wondered if perhaps it wouldn't alarm him.''

"Tip him off, somehow, you mean?"

"Well, not exactly that. The sale is, after all, a matter of public record. What interests me is what that young man thought he would be doing with the place. Afterward, you know. He must have had a plan.''

''Ah,'' said George. ''I declare you're right about that, Dewey.''

''George—what would you say to paying a call on Bruce Ward?''

''Bruce? Why?''

''I'd have a feeling that he may have some information.''

''Well, surely he would have told Booker everything he knows about the affair, Dewey. And I know for a fact that he as been most cooperative in the investigation.''

''Yes, I'm sure he has, George—but do you think Bookie knows the right questions to be asking?''

''Ah.'' George thought about this. ''Good point. I don't suppose you're going to tell me what you have in mind?''

''When I have thought it through some more, I will. You should be able to think of it yourself, anyway, George. Will you help me out?''

''Certainly, my dear. Anything you like. Tonight?''

''Oh, no. Tomorrow will do. You set it up, will you? And then call me. I'll be at the library all morning, but perhaps we can see him for lunch in Leesburg, if he's free.''

''Righto, Captain,'' said George with a twinkle. ''And— since we don't have to go sleuthing tonight—what would you say to a dish of ice cream?'' He went to the freezer and pulled out a carton of butter pecan ice cream. It was Dewey's favorite, he knew. ''With or without chocolate sauce, my dear?''

Dewey James didn't answer. She was deep in thought.

22

OWEN BENNET, WHEN Booker and Fenton finally got their hands on him, proved as cooperative in his second interview as he had been in the first. He had led the two men on a merry chase up and down the winding streets and muddy landings of Canalside, the dark and sparsely populated area on the other side of Adams Bridge. After an exhausting pursuit through narrow alleys and abandoned warehouses, Fenton had managed to catch up with him at the end of the rotting pier known as Fishcake's Wharf.

Now, after half an hour of questioning his chief suspect, Fielding Booker was fit to be tied. He was still closeted with Bennet in the small interrogation room at the back of the police station. Bennet—who appeared sober and not a bit frightened—had dodged all of Booker's questions with an airy superiority that the good police captain would have found trying under the best of circumstances. Which these most decidedly were not.

"You refuse to say what you were doing on the bridge, sir?" asked the police captain with exaggerated courtesy.

"None of your business, Booker. I've told you so." Bennet leaned back in the chair and squared his shoulders. "If you're not going to charge me, I suggest you let me go."

"Oh, I'm going to charge you, all right."

"Is that so?" Bennet seemed amused. "With what?"

"Well, let me see now," said Booker in a patient voice. "For starters, we have creating a public nuisance and resisting arrest. Then there's assault on a police officer—"

"I never touched your sergeant."

"No, but you threw a brick at him. That will do for now, I suppose. And of course, when we retrieve the shell box from the river, there will be an additional charge."

"Hah!" laughed Bennet. The look of amusement on his face caused Booker a momentary misgiving, but he was not to be dissuaded.

"That's right, sir. An additional charge." He rose and bellowed for his sergeant. "Fenton!"

"Sir," replied Fenton briskly, appearing in the doorway.

"Charge this man."

"Yessir."

He counted out the charges on his fingers. "We've got creating a public nuisance. Resisting arrest. Assault." Booker strode mightily to the door and turned once more to glower at Bennet. "And while you're at it, Mikey, write out a summons for littering. That's a two-hundred-dollar summons in Hamilton, sir. Good evening to you."

Booker retreated to his office, where a large bottle of antacid was waiting, and shut the door firmly.

Shoemaker had been dispatched to rouse Judge Baker to obtain a search warrant; and divers would be sent, at the morning's first light, to scour the area beneath the bridge. Booker would call in dredgers if necessary; but there was little hope, indeed, of recovering the shell box. The river under Adams Bridge was tricky and deep. They might have to wait until the spring, Booker reflected sourly, as he took a large swig of pink antacid medicine, when the waters rushed mightily and spewed their bounty of lost items up on the riverbanks. For now, however, everything rested on getting the man to open up. He leaned back in his chair and contemplated his strategy.

There was a knock at the door.

"Come," said Booker fiercely.

"Sir?" Officer Shoemaker stuck her head around the door.

"Yes, Shoemaker?" snapped Booker, annoyed. He felt that he was on the verge of cracking this case; but he needed to be left alone, to think things through in a precise and intense fashion. It would do him no good to have to answer questions from his rookies all night long.

"Sir, this report just came in on the fax." She waved a paper at him, half timidly. Fielding Booker, as his staff well knew, loathed the fax machine, distrusting its transmissions as deeply as if they came from Mars or Moscow.

Officer Shoemaker had another reason to feel timid. She knew that Bennet was being charged in the back room; but the news she had just received might upset the applecart. Being, however, a smart and capable young woman, determined to make detective one day, Officer Shoemaker bit the bullet and put the paper down on the desk. Fielding Booker scowled at it, then sat up straight in his chair.

"Great Scott!" he thundered. "Where did this come from?"

"The Leesburg police sent it. They just had a report from the people at Mackenzie Munitions." She cleared her throat. "It was one of their make, sir. So even though it had never been registered, we were able to trace it through the maker."

"This is not what I expected," grumbled Booker. "Look here, Officer—not a word about this to anyone."

"No, sir."

"I'm serious, now. Don't you go babbling to all your women friends."

Kate Shoemaker held her tongue. She could hardly blame Booker; the news about the shotgun didn't fit in very well with the case he was building.

Booker picked up the paper and glowered at it once more. He didn't like what he saw there; worse still, it confused him.

"French," offered Kate Shoemaker, "was Charlotte Hastings's name. You know, before she got married."

"I am well aware of that fact, young lady. You are dismissed."

"Yes, sir."

Booker tossed the paper down on the desk with disgust.

The gun that had killed Harrison Powell—or whoever the blasted corpse was—had been sold, ten years ago, to Charlotte French. It had been custom-made for her; there could be no mistake about it. The gunsmith at Mackenzie who had made it was now dead, but his widow, when she was finally reached and interviewed, remembered the weapon particularly. It had been the last shotgun that her husband had designed; and the walnut for the butt had come from a tree on their property—one of the last great black walnuts in the county.

This turn of events was quite a blow, indeed, for Captain

Fielding Booker. He reached for the telephone with a sigh and dialed the Leesburg police.

Booker spoke briefly with the Leesburg police and then telephoned Bruce Ward, who had done the research on the gun at Mackenzie Munitions. Ward—who was also the senior hunting guide at Marshy Point—had agreed to come over the next day to make certain of the identification; but he left little doubt that the shotgun was the same one that had been made for Charlotte Hastings, née French, a decade before.

Late that evening Booker made his way once more to the rectory. As he seated himself in the crowded study, he made no apology for calling so late; nor did Charlotte Hastings, when she had heard the reason for the visit, seem to think any apology was necessary. She put aside her knitting and gave Booker her full attention, picking nervously at the arm of the sofa while he talked.

Cedric, roused from his perusal of a philosophical journal, sat perfectly still in his armchair. A small book was open on his lap, and his reading glasses were perched on his nose; he seemed to be having a difficult time wresting his thoughts from the slim volume before him—it was Ross's proof of the existence of God. The merits of the argument, a favorite subject of debate between himself and Dan Powell, had never ceased to fascinate Hastings; in times of personal difficulty he turned to it, the way some people turn to *Pride and Prejudice* for comfort. Fielding Booker, however, didn't know this, and he found the rector's air of distraction irritating in the extreme.

"This is a very grave situation, Mrs. Hastings," said Booker with feeling. "We have confirmation from the state lab and from the Leesburg police that the murder weapon is your property. Do you have any idea how it came to be at the Ducking Club?"

Charlotte Hastings shook her head and looked earnestly at Booker. "None, Captain. That is—"

"Did you sell it? Give it away? Lend it out?"

She shook her head. "No. That is—I can't remember the last time I saw it—not with any certainty."

"Where did you keep it?" asked Booker, addressing them both. Cedric appeared hardly to notice the question. Indeed, he seemed utterly unperturbed by the strange arrival of the police at his home at this late hour. Booker found the dismissive complacency in his manner unnerving; but the good policeman, mindful of his duty to Society, was determined not to be undone by the disconcerting calm of the clergyman. He looked sternly at Charlotte French and awaited her answer.

"Oh! You see, Captain, we *had* kept it in the attic. Until the end of October, thereabouts. Isn't that right, Cedric?"

Hastings looked up from his book and regarded his wife with an air of mild absentmindedness. "Whatever you say, dear. You know perfectly well that I didn't touch the thing."

"No, you didn't. But you must remember when we took it over."

"Just a minute," interposed Booker. "You're telling me you took this gun to the church?"

"That's right, Captain," replied Charlotte, beginning to appear more relaxed. "We had decided to sell it."

"Ah," said Booker, finally grasping the situation. "You were selling it at the church auction."

"That's right. The auction was the third Saturday in October, two weeks before the concert."

"Who bid on it?"

Charlotte shook her head. "It wasn't part of the regular bidding—it was in the silent auction. You know—where people write their names down in a little book." She glanced anxiously at her husband. "I thought it might be awkward for Cedric, you know—to be selling firearms. But we wanted to be rid of it. The silent auction seemed like the best solution."

"Well, then. The buyer's name will be in the records." Booker sounded gratified. This was going to be a snap. He would lay odds that Owen Bennet's name would appear in that little book.

"The gun didn't sell," said Charlotte flatly. She glanced unhappily toward Cedric. "My husband doesn't know this—but I had put in a reserve." Cedric looked sharply at his wife, but his face remained impassive.

"A what?" asked Booker. These people were beginning to get on his nerves. Auctioning off lethal weapons at a church!

"You know—a minimum bid." The admission was clearly awkward for Charlotte Hastings. She sounded, for the first time, slightly defensive. "Well—that gun meant something to me. I was attached to it. And Harrison—whoever he was—he and I agreed that it was worth quite a lot of money, you know. It was made especially for me.''

"Yes, so I have heard," rumbled Booker.

"I didn't want it going to someone who couldn't appreciate it. So I put in a reserve of a thousand dollars.''

Booker raised a brow. That was quite a lot of money for anything at the Good Shepherd auction. "And no one met your price, I take it.''

"That's right." Charlotte kept her eyes on Booker.

"I see." Booker stroked his chin and looked from Charlotte Hastings to her husband, who was regarding his wife sternly. Booker went on. "And, when the auction was over, you simply left it on the premises?''

"Yes," Charlotte answered quickly. "I thought about bringing it home, but I knew that would upset Cedric. So I left it there, in the storeroom upstairs next to the music room. It seemed a logical thing to do at the time. There were some shells, too, in the case, but it wasn't loaded, and the case had a lock.''

"What kind of shells?''

"For big game." Charlotte looked uneasily toward her husband.

"Well, now, Mrs. Hastings." Things were not shaping up to Fielding Booker's liking. The woman was clearly on the defensive; it was time for him to take off the gloves. "I seem to recall that you were quite a shot in your day.''

Charlotte nodded. "But that has nothing—''

"Which is why, of course, you owned such a gun in the first place.''

"Really, Captain," said Cedric, his voice icy. "My wife's childhood hobbies have nothing to do with this business.''

"On the contrary, Cedric," replied Booker with equanimity. "It would seem they have everything to do with it. The murder weapon, after all, belonged to her.''

"Yes, but anyone could have got his hands on it." Booker's questions were finally beginning to rattle the rector's icy composure. He looked sternly at Booker, a dangerous calm fury in his eyes. "The whole town must have known that the gun was for sale. I would appreciate it if you would leave my wife and myself out of it. We don't traffic in weapons." Cedric sniffed.

"On the contrary, Cedric," Booker pointed out with elaborate courtesy. "On the contrary—that is precisely what you were doing. As a matter of fact, I shall be obliged to look into the rules governing such a transfer of arms. In the meantime, however, suppose you tell me something else."

"Yes?" asked Charlotte, sounding eager. "Whatever we can tell you, Captain, we will."

"Very good, Mrs. Hastings. All right, then. How many people realized, after the auction, that the gun had not sold?"

"Why—anyone who had been there, I suppose. The bidding book was open on the little table in the common room. And I think it was there for quite a while. Don't you, Cedric?"

Cedric ignored her question and looked at Booker. "Good heavens, Bookie. Did you come here to offend us? The whole congregation probably knew."

There was silence in the room, punctuated by burbling noises from the aerator in Cedric's fish tank. Fielding Booker found himself staring hard at the fish. This was a mess, all right. The murder weapon had been traced to the dead man's closest associates in town. But Fielding Booker, once he had got hold of an idea, was not a man to give up.

"And the choir members?"

"Why don't you ask them, Bookie?" snapped Hastings.

"I shall, Cedric, I shall. But for now I am asking you. Do you suppose, for example, that Owen Bennet knew?"

"Owen?" asked Charlotte. "Oh, come now, Captain, I don't think Owen—"

"Please, don't speculate, Mrs. Hastings. Just answer my questions. Is it likely that he knew about it?"

"Of course he did, Bookie," remarked Cedric tartly. "He helped with the auction arrangements. Didn't he, my dear?"

Charlotte, thus appealed to, hesitated. "I don't remember."

"You remember, Charlotte," said Cedric in a steady voice. "Use your brain, my darling." He looked at Booker. "What is more, Captain, Owen Bennet came to the church the day after the auction to help Julia move the harp. The one Wally Penberry keeps trying to sell. He had offered to put the harp in the storeroom, but it was too large. So he and Powell—Scobey—found a spot for it in the music room." He turned to his wife. "Am I right, my dear?"

"Yes, so he did," conceded Charlotte in a small voice. "So he did."

Booker breathed easily once more. He was on the right track. Now, finally, they would get somewhere with the stubborn Owen Bennet. He would speak to Julia Boucher and have her confirm Bennet's activity on the day after the auction. That information, taken together with Bruce Ward's assertions about the double-buck, gave them everything they needed in the way of circumstantial evidence; now all that was lacking was a motive, and Booker planned to get that from the choir. One among their number would sing, he felt sure. He chuckled to himself at his little mental joke.

"I'll need to see the records from the auction," he said.

"Fine, fine," replied Cedric, waving his hand dismissively. "They're in the church office somewhere. Julia would know." He looked at his watch. "But if you don't mind my saying so, Bookie, it's a little late to be rousing Julia." He picked up his book and situated his glasses firmly on his nose.

Booker nodded. "I agree. We can see to that in the morning, first thing. Well, then." He stood and looked awkwardly at the rector and his wife. "I don't suppose I need to tell you that this discussion is to remain quite confidential."

"We'll keep it as quiet as the grave, Bookie," replied Cedric with a rare attempt at humor.

Booker departed, feeling vindicated.

Charlotte Hastings watched with anxious eyes as he made his way down the front path to his car. She returned quietly to the library, where Cedric was once more absorbed in his reading.

"Cedric?"

"Yes, my dear?" Cedric did not look up from his book.

"Cedric—we must talk about this."

"About what, my dear?"

"The murder of that young man."

Hastings put down his book with a sigh and regarded his wife dispassionately. "I won't say I was pleased to hear about the shenanigans with the gun, Charlotte."

"Yes, I know. But it was my gun, after all, Cedric. I had a right to do what I did."

"You know how I feel about such things. Base sentimentality oughtn't to have a place in your heart, Charlotte. Not where something like a gun is concerned. However, there doesn't seem to be anything we can do. It's a pity you didn't just sell it, or give it away. You shouldn't have left it lying about like that.''

''No.'' Charlotte sat down on the arm of her husband's chair. ''I shouldn't have. You're right about that, Cedric—it was a dangerous and foolish thing to do.'' She looked at him carefully. In the light from the reading lamp, his ordinarily sallow skin had taken on an almost waxy glow. The fine, pale gray curls on his head shone with a little of their former blond luster; Charlotte ran a hand idly through his hair.

''What is it, Charlotte?'' he finally remarked, sounding testy.

She let out a little laugh. ''What is it? Cedric—suppose you tell me?''

''I'm afraid there is nothing to tell you, my sweet.'' With evident reluctance he took her hand, then he gave her a severe look. ''Charlotte, Charlotte. This business has you frightened. You mustn't allow it to get to you in this way. Everything will be just fine—you wait and see.'' He kissed her hand idly, then let it drop and took up his book once more.

Charlotte sighed and stood up. ''I'm taking Ben to the pediatrician tomorrow, Cedric. We won't be in to the church office until late.''

''Fine, my dear.''

Charlotte shivered slightly as she left the cozy warmth of the library and made her way through the chill darkness toward the kitchen. She flipped on the overhead light; in its harsh glow she could see Eddie the cat, crouched in an attitude of enormous patience beneath Pindar's cage. As the light came on, the cat blinked once at Charlotte and then leapt, with vicious determination, for the bird.

''*Thanatos! Thanatos!*'' Pindar squawked wildly, fluttering madly against the bars of the cage. ''*Thanatos!*''

''And none too soon,'' muttered Charlotte Hastings softly. Then she began, ever so quietly, to cry.

23

THE NEXT MORNING Dewey's patience was thoroughly tested by Tom Campbell as she eagerly awaited George Farnham's telephone call. She knew that she really ought to talk to Booker about the discovery she had made at the county clerk's office; but she reasoned that perhaps Booker would resent her interference less if she had more conclusive facts to relate. At the very least, he might be forced to pay attention to what she said, without giving her a long lecture on interfering with the police.

But the waiting was difficult. "What is it, Tom?" she asked, exasperated, as that young man waved a publisher's catalog at her. "Not those French poetry books again, I hope. We simply can't afford that kind of luxury."

"Mrs. James," said Campbell in a voice filled with a pity for her ignorance. "I really do wish you'd reconsider. Just look at this: the collected poems of Jacques Prévert, in an elegant edition."

Although Campbell had replaced Dewey as Hamilton's head librarian, he had agreed, on taking the job, that Dewey could retain veto power over whatever purchases the library might wish to make. He was now attempting to override. But he might have saved his breath.

"Good heavens, Tom. We've got enough Jacques Prévert to sink a ship. All those old French textbooks that Hamilton High donated. They're loaded with Prévert."

"But these are elegant, calf-bound volumes, Mrs. James."

"I'm sure they are, Tom. But really, do you think it's wise

140

to spend so much money on French poetry for the populace of Hamilton? If you're anxious for French literature, I think Simenon, in translation, is more our style here.''

Dewey knew this argument would appeal to Tom Campbell, who felt the readership at the little library to be woefully lacking in all the best qualities of intellectuality. He had recently begun spouting snippets of philosophy and talking a great deal about the ''life of the mind''; on the whole, Dewey thought that Cedric Hasting's parrot Pindar had a surer grasp of the classical authors.

Dewey had it on the best authority that Tom had been squiring about Andrée Quenelle, the local French teacher—which accounted not only for his newfound love of French poetry, but also for his trip to France. Well, thought Dewey, he and Andrée Quenelle were more or less of the same kidney. She choked back a laugh and gave Campbell a wide-eyed look.

''Tom—what do you know about hunting?''

''Hunting?'' Campbell looked dismayed. ''Nothing. Absolutely nothing. I detest blood sports.''

''Do you, now?'' replied Dewey. ''Well, I suppose you have a point—in light of the tragic accident out at the Marshy Point.''

''Yes, indeed, I have a point,'' replied Campbell. ''But that was no accident, Mrs. James. In fact, I'm rather surprised that you have time for the library, with a murderer on the loose in town. In fact, a regular crime wave. What with the burglary of the Music Society's receipts, followed almost immediately by a murder, I'm surprised you find time even to sleep at night.'' Tom Campbell fiercely disapproved of Dewey's intervention in local crime detection. His disapprobation caused Dewey much amusement.

''Yes—well, I hope our good Captain Booker isn't off after the wrong fox. It wouldn't be the first time. But you know, Tom, you have put me in mind of something. I don't suppose you have any suspicion of who might have robbed the church the day of the concert?''

''I should hope not,'' sniffed Campbell, and he resumed his perusal of the French publisher's catalog.

Dewey was rescued from Campbell's high-mindedness by the telephone. It was George Farnham; Bruce Ward had agreed to meet them if they could come to the Mackenzie Munitions offices in Leesburg at lunchtime.

"I'll call for you at twelve-fifteen, if I may," said Farnham. "That is, if I'm allowed to tag along on this adventure of yours."

"That would be most kind of you, George."

"Don't you want to give me a hint what this is about, my dear?" asked Farnham plaintively.

"George. Be patient, please." Dewey glowered at Tom Campbell, who was waving another catalog under her nose. "I must go." She lowered her voice to a whisper. "Tom wants to enlarge our French literature section."

"Great Scott!" George exclaimed. "Hasn't gotten over his trip to the Côte d'Azur yet?"

"*Exactement,*" responded Dewey in her best French. "*A bientôt.*"

"Let him eat cake," said George with a chuckle and rang off.

At precisely one o'clock Dewey and George arrived at the sleek glass building in Leesburg that houses the offices of Mackenzie Munitions. The gunworks were on the other side of town; several years ago, however, old Stewart Mackenzie (who had a very sharp eye for the main chance) had landed a contract for building replicas of antiques for a large movie studio. Revenues had quadrupled, and the company executives had moved into this late-model mini-skyscraper.

Within these bland modern surroundings, however, the company had maintained its frontier-style, Daniel-Boone flavor. There were hunting prints on every wall of the main lobby, and the handset of the receptionist's telephone was a perfect polymer imitation of an eighteenth-century dueling pistol. Old Stewart Mackenzie had a one-track mind.

Bruce Ward greeted them in the lobby and led them down the corridor to his office. The engineer and George Farnham were old buddies; Dewey James he knew less well, but he had always found her company agreeable, and he seemed thrilled that she had come to call.

"I ordered up some sandwiches for us," said Ward, his boyish blue eyes twinkling. "I thought it might be a good idea, since you said it was confidential, George. The company cafeteria's got big ears." He raised an eyebrow and looked with interest at Dewey. He knew this was her show. "You're kind of a famous person, even in Leesburg, Mrs. James."

"Well, Bruce—it was thoughtful of you to order lunch," remarked Dewey as she settled herself in one of his visitors' chairs and looked about.

Ward's office was large and spacious. On every available surface there was a weapon of some sort—an antique flintlock rifle here, an ivory-handled derringer there. In one corner, looking oddly impotent, was a Gatling gun. It was hard for Dewey to conceive that such an outmoded-looking weapon could have so ravaged the forces of troops who had marched against it. There was something pitiful about the thing now— but, thought Dewey, all such weapons were pitiful. Such were the lessons of history. Why had they never learned? As she looked about her, she could understand Cedric Hastings's reluctance to sell his family estate to the company. There was something decidedly unsettling in the air.

"I hope you like ham and Swiss," Ward went on.

"I adore ham and Swiss, and so does George. Don't you, George?"

George, taking the other chair, was impatient. "Come now, my dear. We didn't come here to eat. Suppose you tell us poor mortals what you've got in mind."

"Yes, indeed," replied Dewey. She glanced at Ward, who had settled himself behind his desk and put his feet up.

"I sure hope you didn't come out here on some wild-goose chase, Mrs. James. I don't really know what I can tell you that the police don't already know, but old George here said you were determined to come. I told Captain Booker everything I know about the day of the murder. Except for the report on the shotgun, of course. Didn't get the report until yesterday."

"The gun?" Dewey sat up straight. "Good heavens, you mean the murder weapon?"

"Uh-oh," said Ward with a smile. "I don't want to let the cat out of the bag, Mrs. James."

"No, surely not," said Dewey firmly, a twinkle in her eye. "On the other hand, if the report on the gun will soon be common knowledge, you might as well let us in on it." She smiled benignly upon Ward, who laughed aloud in response.

"Fielding Booker will have my head if he knows I told you. Can you keep it dark?"

"By all means," replied George Farnham, all ears. "Dark as night. Let me guess—it was one of yours?"

"Got it in one, George. Made to order."

"For whom?" asked Dewey. Ward shot her a look.

"Don't rightly know as I ought to say, Mrs. James."

"Oh, come now, Bruce. The whole company is probably talking about it by now. Wouldn't you think?"

"I suppose you have a point." He pulled at an earlobe and looked at them thoughtfully. "Cedric Hastings's wife."

"Ah," said Dewey. "Well—that doesn't make it simple for the police, I assure you. Charlotte Hastings sold that gun." She turned to George. "It was part of the silent bidding at the auction, George. You remember."

"Can't say I remember, Dewey, since I didn't attend the auction. But I'll take it on faith."

"Yes. Well, take it on faith, then. That is most interesting news. Most interesting, indeed," she said thoughtfully. "I wonder if Charlotte knows the police have traced the murder weapon to her?" she asked Ward.

"Don't know about that, Mrs. James. Only just got the report in and phoned the Leesburg police with it like I was supposed to. Shoot, I hope I haven't loused anything up. But Booker didn't say to keep it a secret or anything."

"Don't you worry, Bruce. We won't, er, split on you. Will we, George?"

"We wouldn't dream of splitting on you," asserted George with feeling.

"All right, then. I guess that makes it okay with me." Ward smiled again at Dewey. "Well, ma'am, looks like I've been monopolizing our little visit. Was there something else you wanted to talk to me about?"

"Yes, there was. Well"—Dewey took a breath—"it wasn't about the day of the murder that I wanted to inquire, Bruce," she answered. "In fact, I was rather hoping to ask you to do a little industrial spying for me. About the property."

"Marshy Point?"

Dewey shook her head. "The Hastings property. Which Cedric had wanted to sell. Mackenzie Munitions, you may recall, had put in a bid for it."

"So we did," Ward acknowledged. "You know, I forgot all about that. I told old man Mackenzie that his bid would never be accepted, but he thinks Cedric is full of fiddlesticks—that's what he called it—'fiddlesticks and twaddle.'"

"Oh, my," said Dewey mildly. "He doesn't know our Cedric very well, does he?"

Ward shook his head. "Nope. He was pretty near convinced he could get the good reverend to change his mind, if he upped the bid. Said he never knew a churchman who didn't like money."

"And did he? Up the bid, that is."

Ward nodded. "Doubled it."

"Good heavens." Dewey was filled with admiration for Cedric's fortitude—although she couldn't help thinking that the resulting Elder Care House might have justified his relenting on his principles, just this once. "Well?"

Ward laughed. "Cedric sent our attorney packing. Gave him a long lecture about Gandhi and pacifism, which the guy had to sit there and take. And, when he got back here—the lawyer, that is—he had to repeat it, word for word, to old Mackenzie. The old man was furious—turned bright red and stomped all around, hollering at everyone in sight. That was a day to remember!"

"But why on earth did Mr. Mackenzie want the Hastings Place so badly?"

Ward shrugged. "I don't think he did, at first. Somebody said maybe we ought to buy it, use it as a corporate retreat, take our clients out there shooting. He thought it sounded like a good idea—nice countryside, not too far from home. But then, when Cedric wouldn't sell, old man Mackenzie decided he couldn't live without it." He chuckled. "Well—you know how people are sometimes."

"I do, indeed," agreed Dewey warmly. She was familiar with this particular strain of acquisitiveness, which she found perfectly comprehensible and yet distasteful in the extreme. Stewart Mackenzie was a colorful and rather ruthless man, famous for getting what he wanted.

"Dewey," George interrupted. "Forgive me—but what on earth has this got to do with Clyde Scobey?"

"Oh," said Dewey with a smile. "Everything, I think. Or almost everything."

"What do you mean, everything? Dewey—you can't think old man Mackenzie had him killed?" George shook his head. Maybe some of the town wags were right; maybe Dewey was losing her grip.

She dismissed him with a wave. "Don't be an idiot, George. Please." She turned her gaze once more to Ward. "Then what happened?"

"Ah," said Ward. "Well—I don't rightly know, you see. I was out of town for a couple weeks, me and my family. On vacation. But when I got back, I did hear some rumblings about the Hastings place. How we were going to get it anyway. Then that fellow Powell—or I guess I should say Scobey—called me about membership in the Marshy Point. And then I thought maybe I was wrong. Because he told me he had bought the place himself."

"He called you, did he?"

"Yep. He was nice enough, but he let me know that he had something cooking with the big cheese here. And that, as a kindness to myself, I ought to propose him for membership. Like there might be something in it for me, somehow. I couldn't figure it, but he seemed nice enough."

"Dewey—"

"Hush, George. Bruce—did you have any idea what he meant?"

"You know, I must be awful slow. He was dropping hints left and right, on the morning of the day he was killed, about having some sweet deal in the offing. But I'm kind of a simple guy, Mrs. James. I had no idea he had swindled old Cedric. I thought he was supposed to be Cedric's friend."

"So did we all. He was most convincing, that young man. Listen, Bruce—can you find out for us the terms of the arrangement? Did the sale go through, do you think?"

"Now, wait a minute, you two," put in Farnham solidly. "Just hold your horses, and allow poor old George to catch up. Dewey, you're saying that Powell made a deal with Mackenzie to sell the place to them after all?"

"I believe so, George."

"Why, that detestable scoundrel!" Farnham was scandalized.

"He was a con artist, after all," Dewey reminded him gently. "I suppose it came naturally to him."

"Yeah," Ward concurred. "He was pretty damned smooth, that character. He told me, on that Saturday morning, that he expected to be in Leesburg on Monday. So I guess that was the idea."

"Why on earth hasn't anyone come forward with this information?" Farnham looked sternly at Ward, who shrugged his shoulders.

"Like I said, George—I just hadn't pieced it together. Not the way Mrs. James has. I thought he was just a kid, talking big. And since the day he died, there hasn't been any mention of the corporate retreat. I figured old man Mackenzie just found him another rabbit to chase after and kind of forgot about it. He does that, these days. Getting kind of past it, like some old hound. He can't keep one idea in his head for more'n about five minutes."

"Dear me," said Dewey.

"Well?" Ward smiled brightly. "Sandwiches, everybody?"

As they drove back to Hamilton, George Farnham questioned Dewey closely. Bruce Ward had promised to do a little digging about the situation; he would call them if he thought there was something to report. George, no longer mystified, was now feeling that he had made a rather poor showing as a detective. Dewey and Ward had talked circles around him. He comforted himself with the thought that Dewey had made a fortunate guess.

"Come now, my dear. That was just a shot in the dark, and you know it. You were very lucky that Bruce was so ready to talk."

"Pish-tosh, George. It was a carefully reasoned deduction from the facts. And if you hadn't been so busy being pleased with yourself, you would have thought of it yourself."

"Reasoned? How, reasoned?" George was miffed. He hated having to ask Dewey to explain herself.

"Well, just look at the situation, George—but you have to look at it from back to front, if you want it to be logical."

"Thank you, Aristotle. Or should I say Alice?"

"Don't be snide. You're just jealous, that's all. Settle down and listen to me. When that young man was Harrison Powell, it made some kind of sense for him to wish to settle in Hamilton, near an old family friend—he's an orphan, remem-

ber. It made sense for him to immerse himself in the life of our
little community—to join the choir and make friends with
people. Even, for that matter, to make an enemy of Owen
Bennet. Because that's what people do—they make friends and
enemies.''

''Hmm,'' said George, keeping his eyes firmly fixed on the
road.

''On the other hand, once you know that the young man was
not Harrison Powell—that he was, in fact, a con artist—then
you have to begin to wonder what his—er—game was going to
be. If you are using any kind of logic at all.''

''Yes, I see,'' agreed George. ''When you know it's not
Powell, but Scobey, then you have to try to figure his angle.''

''Precisely.'' Dewey reached over and patted George's arm.
''You're catching on. Well, now. The only article of value
which that young man had acquired was Cedric's old family
estate. So there must be something afoot with regard to the old
Hastings place. Everyone in town knew that Cedric had turned
down Mackenzie's offer. It was commonly noised about—an
easy enough item of local interest for Scobey to pick up. And
when you knew that he had pressured Cedric into selling
it—even threatened him, somehow—''

''Whoa, whoa! How do we know that?''

''Because he only paid a hundred dollars for it. And there
must be a reason for that.''

''Ah, yes. I had forgotten your visit to Hilda Beane.''

''Well, just don't you forget it. It was important. And *that*,''
she remarked soothingly, ''*was* rather a shot in the dark. But
not such a bad one.''

''Now who's pleased with herself?'' said George, chuckling
amiably.

''Well, it was clever of me to look at the records, George.
Not to mention brave—facing down Hilda Beane, with her
furious rubber stamping. You have to admit it was brave.''

''So I do, my dear, so I do. You are a remarkably brave and
clever girl. Now—I hate to rain on your parade, but you
haven't solved the murder case yet, you know.''

''Yes, I know,'' replied Dewey in an altogether different
tone of voice.

''Do you think that Powell was killed just to stop the sale to
Mackenzie?''

"It's certainly possible," said Dewey. "The thing we must discover now, I suppose, is who might have known about his double-dealing."

"Hmm." They drove in silence for some time, thinking through the possibilities.

"I guess I had better go and talk to Bookie, George," remarked Dewey at last as they entered Hamilton.

"Yes—I'll drop you at the police station. Would you like me to come in with you, my dear? Run interference with our Lion of the Law?"

Dewey laughed. "I wouldn't want to get you in any hot water, George, thank you. And it may be useful to have an ally that the police don't suspect of sabotaging their case. I'll leave you out of it, if you like."

"Leave me out?" George sounded hurt.

"Or include you," amended Dewey hastily.

"Please, Dewey dear. You know how much I love it when you include me." They pulled up before the police station. George smiled sweetly at Dewey and gave the car horn a couple of toots. "Count me in, my dear," he said, planting a kiss on her cheek. "Count me in through thick and thin."

24

Poor Fielding Booker! Alas, Hamilton's great Lion of the Law, as George Farnham had dubbed him, was about to have his claws pared—and not for the first time—by the redoubtable Dewey James.

He wasn't aware of the comeuppance that awaited him, however; and while George and Dewey were making their triumphant way back from Leesburg, he was closeted once more in the police interrogation room with the unfortunate Owen Bennet.

Bennet, it must be said, was the author of much of his own discomfort. He had always been one of those people who make things as difficult as possible for themselves; this was true in his relations with the ladies of Hamilton (and their wrathful husbands), and in his stubborn propensity to drink far too much and far too often.

In the investigation of the murder of Clyde Scobey, he had likewise dug himself into a hole—through his supercilious refusal to cooperate with the police. If he had been straightforward with Booker from the beginning, he would never have been the good captain's chief suspect; even Fielding Booker could let go of a bad idea when he clearly understood its weakness. But there it was: Bennet reveled in attention and always knew how to place himself firmly at the center of controversy. Thus, he found himself once more bearing up under the unflinching gaze and the awful questioning of Captain Fielding Booker.

"I have it on the authority of an unimpeachable witness, sir, that you knew of the presence of the gun in that storeroom," Booker rumbled. "You saw the shotgun there on the day following the church auction."

"If you say so," remarked Bennet.

"I don't need to say so, Bennet, when I have got an eyewitness. You saw the gun when you attempted to place Mr. Penberry's harp in the storage area."

Bennet yawned. "Yes, Captain, you are absolutely right."

"Well, then," said Booker, leaning heavily across the table and looking Bennet squarely in the eye. "Do you propose, sir, to tell me that your ready access to the murder weapon has no bearing on this case?"

"I don't propose to tell you anything, Captain Booker, except that I would very much like to go home."

"Would you, now?"

"Indeed. Listen, Booker," said Bennet, beginning to show strain in the proceedings. It had been fun to bait the credulous Fielding Booker; but the amusement was beginning to wear thin. "This will do you no good, no good at all. I strongly suggest that for your own peace of mind you give up this foolish idea of yours and track down the real criminal. Whoever he is."

"Well, now," said Booker in a tone of mocking gratitude, "we all thank you for your consideration, sir. But let me tell you that I have got evidence—good, solid evidence—in this matter.

"Number one: You had quarreled with the deceased man, in the presence of witnesses; he had humiliated you before your neighbors, friends, and fellow musicians. You were not only nursing a grievance, but you had allowed that grievance to so overtake your good sense that you assaulted him and threatened him, with no provocation, in a public place and before witnesses.

"Number two: You refuse to communicate your whereabouts at the time of the murder. Nor will you furnish any kind of witness to your own innocence of the crime.

"Number three: My own sergeant and I watched as you attempted to dispose of material evidence—the shell box, which I suspect contains double-buck of the sort used to murder Clyde Scobey. Bruce Ward remembers selling you double-buck from the Marshy Point munitions store just two weeks before the murder was committed. However, we shall know more when the divers have finished with that stretch of the Boone River.

"Number four: You had ready access to the murder weapon. You know your way through the precincts of the church, and as a member of the choir and the Music Society, you frequent the premises where the weapon was stored.

"Now, sir—I give you these facts: motive, means, and opportunity. This is not a trifling matter, and I intend to see that my charge of murder against you, when I file it, sticks."

Throughout this thunderous recital Bennet had kept up his appearance of calm. By the time Booker had finished his dreadful catalog of evidence, however, the good captain had worked himself up to a fine state of frustration and rage. "Do you have nothing to say?" he thundered at last, pounding on the table.

Bennet shook his head. "You have missed your calling, Captain. You ought to have been a prosecuting attorney. And, speaking of attorneys, I should very much like to call Tony Zimmerman. It's about time I found myself legal representation in this farce."

Booker took this request as a sign that he would prevail and hastily summoned Mike Fenton. "Wants a lawyer, Mike," Booker croaked. His diatribe had left him hoarse. "You handle it, boy, will you? As soon as Zimmerman gets here, book him. Murder One."

"Er, yessir," said Fenton. Booker headed for the door, but Fenton stopped him. "Ah—sir—"

"For the love of Pete, Mikey, what is it?"

"It's Mrs. James, sir. She's in the waiting room out front, with Mr. Farnham."

"Hah!" Booker fairly glowed. "Well, for once our lady detective is a little late on the scene. Hah!" he laughed again and strode forward, in the full flush of victory, to rub the nose of Dewey James in the success of the Hamilton police.

Poor Fielding Booker.

When the three of them were seated in Booker's office, Dewey plunged right in.

"I know you won't want to hear any of this, Bookie, but there are just a few facts that I wanted you to have, before anything, er, untoward develops. You know what I mean?'' She gestured with her head toward the back of the police station. Officer Shoemaker had let drop the interesting fact that Owen Bennet was in the interrogation room.

Booker, who was by now sucking on a throat lozenge, beamed at her with unusual receptiveness. ''Fine, Dewey, fine. We've got our case, you know. Suspect's in the back, about to be booked for Murder One. But if you have anything useful to tell me, I'm sure we will appreciate it.''

Uh-oh, thought George Farnham. They might be too late to rescue Booker from his own folly. Owen Bennet was not above suing the police for false arrest, if it came to that. He hoped they would be in time to save the town the expense of a lawsuit.

Dewey went firmly ahead. ''Bookie, we have been to see Bruce Ward at Mackenzie Munitions.''

''Have you, now?''

''Yes,'' she replied firmly, giving her silvery curls a defiant toss. ''And he has confirmed something that I suspected. Clyde Scobey had made a deal to sell Cedric's old homestead to Stewart Mackenzie.''

''Whoa, wait a minute, now, Dewey. Hold on. Cedric didn't even sell the place to Scobey—so what difference does it make? The sale was a fraud. Null and void. And I've got bigger fish to fry.''

''Well, yes—you do. And we know now that the sale was a fraud, because the man is dead and we know who he was. But let me tell you, Bookie, that he might just have pulled it off.'' And she related to him everything that she had discovered, including the astonishing purchase price for which Cedric had sold his family place and its thirty-two acres of prime real estate. When she reached the end of her tale, Booker was thoroughly confused.

''You mean to tell me that Cedric Hastings sold that place to a con man for a hundred dollars?'' He shook his head. ''I'm sorry, Dewey, but I can't believe it. Even if Cedric weren't the most tightfisted pinchpenny that ever decorated a pulpit, I wouldn't credit that. It doesn't make any sense.''

''Bookie, you're looking at it backwards. He wasn't selling the place to a con man—or he didn't think of it that way. He was selling it to a young man who, having lost his own father, had turned up on his doorstep. A young man, I may say, whose existence seemed to trouble him in some way.''

''Trouble him?''

''Yes.'' Dewey nodded significantly and turned rather pink. ''I did have a look at those pictures of Cedric's—the ones from Kerangani. The young man who turned up here, calling himself Harrison Powell, didn't look a thing like his father. He had his mother's golden hair and blue eyes—but you know, he didn't really look like either Dan or Lucy Powell. Hardly surprising, now that we know who he was. But I think he planted a seed of anxiety in Cedric's mind.''

''Anxiety?'' Booker still didn't understand. Dewey was going to have to spell it out for the policeman; George sat back comfortably to watch.

''Uneasiness. He upset Cedric in some way—Charlotte told me so, only a week before the boy died. And I think I know the reason why.''

''I'm sure you do, Dewey. You always seem to know absolutely everything.''

''Bookie—Cedric Hastings was in love with Lucy Powell. Now, I'm not saying this is so; but you know, things do happen between people. That young man was born shortly after the Powells returned home from Kerangani. I think he had some-how suggested to Cedric that—that Cedric might be hard pressed to demonstrate, if it came to it, that he was not himself the boy's father.''

''Oh, come now, Dewey, you are leaping to conclusions again. Romantic speculation.'' Booker waved the notion away. It was absurd.

''I may be speculating, Bookie—but I saw the pictures of the Powells and of Cedric in Kerangani. I talked to Charlotte, as well. Something happened between Cedric and Lucy, out in Kerangani, twenty-five years ago—of that there can be no doubt at all. I tried to ask Cedric about it—''

''Oh, Dewey, really. That was going too far, even for you.'' Booker was shocked by her temerity. ''You didn't really ask him?''

''Well, not straight out,'' Dewey admitted. ''I more or less gave him a chance to discuss it with me. But, Bookie, you must see it. Cedric tossed away the chance to realize his own dream—the funding of the Elder Care House—and sold his family place for a nominal sum. Can you offer an explanation?''

Booker sat back in his chair and thought hard about it. ''I have to admit there is something in that,'' he said, with deep reluctance, at last. ''Yes, Dewey. Confound it.'' He glared at her. ''Are you suggesting that the young man exacted the house as some kind of blackmail payment?''

''Well, it did rather strike me that way. Only I imagine he phrased it rather eloquently—probably he suggested that Cedric might like to make the purchase easy for him, in a gesture to his departed friends Dan and Lucy.''

''What a scoundrel,'' said Booker sadly. ''I suppose I ought to thank you for bringing this information to my attention, Dewey.'' He glanced involuntarily toward the back of the police station, where even now Mike Fenton might be in the process of formalizing charges against Owen Bennet. ''We may have to rethink this one.'' He got up and strode to the door. ''Fenton!'' he roared.

Mike Fenton appeared at the door. ''Sir? We're still waiting for Tony Zimmerman to get here.''

''Just wait, then, will you? When he gets here. Don't do anything else, just wait.''

Fenton raised a brow and looked from his captain to Dewey James. The old lady had done it again, thought Fenton ruefully. It was just too bad that Booker wouldn't listen to her advice from the beginning of a case—they could avoid this sort of scene if he would pay attention to her crazy notions from the start. He really ought to make her an honorary member of the crime squad.

Fenton knew better than to make any kind of smart remark, however. At moments like this his captain's ego required very delicate handling, indeed. He merely said, ''Yessir,'' and disappeared again down the corridor.

Booker looked sternly from Dewey to George Farnham and back again.

''I'm surprised at both of you. And I don't have to tell you how dangerous this kind of meddling can be, Dewey.''

George sighed. ''Come off it, Bookie. All we did was go for a drive in the countryside and have lunch with a friend.''

''Don't play me for a fool, George, please.'' Booker glowered at him.

"Well, Bookie," put in Dewey soothingly, "at least you can let poor Owen Bennet go."

"How on earth—?" spluttered Booker, but George stepped in.

"Well, he was the most obvious suspect in the case. Not hard to prove he had a grudge against the dead man. Nobody will hold it against you, Booker."

"Oh, and I guess you think I ought to be grateful for that?" replied Booker sourly. "We can still charge him with creating a public nuisance."

"You would have done that a long time ago, if some of the wronged husbands in town had been given a say in it," said George with a chuckle.

"I suppose you have a point," responded Booker. He was beginning to recover his good spirits. Dewey's intervention had saved him from a costly mistake. He grew more somber in a moment, however, as he reflected on the nature of her revelations.

"Dewey, I don't want you going any further in this business. It's a damned messy affair, if you ask me, and there isn't going to be much room to maneuver. We will find ourselves in a peck of trouble if we aren't careful. Got to play this thing mighty close to the chest, you know. Need professionals for that sort of thing. Calls for kid gloves, and experienced handling of delicate matters of town opinion." He looked at her sharply. "Do I have your word?"

"On what, Bookie?"

"Oh, come now, my old friend. It's high time you stopped trying to pull the wool over my eyes with that innocent look of yours. I am grateful," he said, rising, "that you have come to me with this information. Speculative as it is, the news you have brought bears looking into. But I don't want anyone else in town sniffing round the rectory to find out about Cedric Hasting's past. You leave that to me. You, too, George. Understood?"

"Of course, Bookie. I wouldn't dream of interfering," replied Dewey easily. She and George took their leave, passing Mike Fenton in the corridor as they made their way out. Dewey gave him a broad wink. The loyal sergeant smiled back at her. She had probably saved the old man's skin once again.

Having thus enjoined Dewey James to silence and inaction, the forces of the Hamilton Police set about their task. Fenton was summoned immediately and brought up to date with the situation.

"So you think this means Owen Bennet didn't do it, sir?"

"Don't know for sure, Mikey. But there's one thing I can tell you. This information throws a new light on the subject."

"Sir."

"That is to say, boy, we must consider it from a different angle. Now, Mrs. James seems to think there's a possibility that Cedric Hastings used to be sweet on Harrison Powell's mother. When they were out in Africa together."

"Yessir."

"And that this fellow Scobey somehow knew this—well, he was a friend of the family, of the Powell family. Went to church with them, sang in the choir, and so forth. That's what Rufus Large told me, you know—the deputy mayor of that town in California where all these miscreants were hatched."

"Gorman's Wood, sir."

"That's the one. Hate California. Anyway, Mike, it strikes me that there could be some truth in the idea. Else why sell the old family place to him for a song?"

"I see your point, sir."

"Do you now? Good. Well done. Let's see, Mike—what kind of information do we have on his whereabouts at the time the murder was committed?"

"Reverend Hastings's whereabouts, sir?"

"Yes, Reverend Hastings. Who'd you think I meant, boy? The corpse? Haha!"

"No, sir. Let me see." Fenton flipped back through his notebook. "He said he paid a call on a sick parishioner. Mrs. Hatfield, sir."

"Well, just you double-check that. Make sure he was at Mrs. Hatfield's place, or otherwise accounted for, between the hours of eleven and noon."

"Yessir." Fenton made a note. "Uh, sir?"

"Yes, Mikey?"

"What about Mrs. Hastings, sir?"

"What about her, Mike?"

"Well, sir—after all, it was her gun that shot the man."

Booker pulled thoughtfully at his chin. "So it was, so it was. Good point. What do your notes say?"

"Umm"—he flipped back some more through the notes— "she was out shopping."

"With the child?"

"No—no, sir. Actually, that was the day my wife, Ellen, took Ben, sir. They had kind of a baby party, my kids and Ben."

"Convenient."

"Yes, sir," replied Fenton, who was not at all sure he liked the idea of his wife furnishing babysitting services to a murderess. "I'll check with Ellen, sir, and see what time they came and left."

"You do that, Mike."

"Anything else?"

"Not for now. Did you tell Bennet he could go?"

Fielding Booker, if the truth be told, was still not convinced that Owen Bennet was innocent of the crime of murder. But he recognized that he would have to answer the questions that Dewey had raised before he could charge the man.

"Yes, sir," Fenton responded. "For the moment, I told him. And I haven't dropped the charge of resisting arrest."

"Good. We'll make that one stick anyway. That man gives me a pain."

"Sir."

25

THE LITTLE TOWN of Hamilton had seen some scandalous behavior in its time, one way and another. But the three or four days that followed the revelations about Harrison Powell and the sale of Cedric Hastings's house rocked the community as nothing in memory had. The revelations seemed to cut at the very heart of civic trust, friendship, and real estate values. Taken in combination, these elements made for a potent brew, indeed—a volatile community cocktail that would lead to reprisal, recrimination, and the general taking of sides. November was shaping up to be a record-breaking month for the local wags.

The events that led up to this orgy of finger-pointing were in themselves rather quiet. Dewey had kept her promise to Fielding Booker, not breathing a word of what she had learned. She fairly burned with curiosity about the murder, and especially longed to know whether Charlotte had sold the gun at the auction or not. But it wouldn't do to go rushing about asking questions of the church staff or the rector and his family; such techniques were like signal flares in a town the size of Hamilton. Dewey determined to abide by her promise to Booker for at least three days.

No, it wasn't Dewey, but Hilda Beane, of all people—the frosty County Clerk—who had set the ball in motion.

Hilda Beane appeared at the Tidal Wave, as was her monthly custom, to update the blue rinse in her hair. Doris Bock was inclined to treat Hilda Beane with great politeness; those in the know accurately ascribed this accommodating behavior to the excess inventory in the back room at the Tidal Wave. Hilda Beane was one of a tiny handful of Hamilton ladies who still blued their hair; but Doris Bock had enough blue rinse to color an army of county clerks. Hence, Doris was careful not to lose Hilda Beane as a customer.

"How goes it at the office of the county clerk?" Doris asked courteously as she lathered Miss Beane.

"Don't even ask," complained that lady. "I have so much work to do, it would make a dog cry. The commissioner promised me five months ago that he would send me a girl, but what does he do? He hires *two* new people for the Leesburg office. I ask you. Is that gratitude? And as if I haven't got enough to do, you people keep coming around, snooping into everybody else's business, and keeping me from my job."

"Goodness!" exclaimed Mary Royce, the publisher of the weekly Hamilton *Quill*. Her reporter's nose scented the makings of a story. "Has someone been snooping, Miss Beane?"

"You people are forever poking your noses in where they don't belong," retorted Hilda Beane. "One after another. Some of you, however, are worse offenders than others."

"Whoever do you mean?" asked Elsie Resnick, who was having a manicure. Elsie as a rule didn't go in for town gossip; but once a month, or thereabouts, she indulged herself at the Tidal Wave, letting the large and small scandals of her hometown wash over her in a soothing wave.

"I'm surprised she hasn't been pestering you, too," Hilda Beane shot back. "After all, you were right there at the scene of the crime. Both of you. If you ask me, Elsie, you all ought to be strung up for not catching Owen Bennet in the act. You were right there, for pity's sake." She shook her head disapprovingly, causing Doris Bock much consternation.

"Please hold still, Miss Beane," Doris reproved her. "How do you know it was Owen Bennet who killed that man?"

"Everyone knows. It's as plain as the nose on your face." Hilda Beane stared meaningfully at Doris Bock's nose, which was admittedly a large apparatus. The gesture was unkind in the extreme, but Doris ignored it.

"Come now, Miss Beane," protested Elsie Resnick. "We all thought it was some kind of accident. We had no idea it was murder. And nobody has said that Owen did it. I, for one, am convinced of his innocence."

"Are you? Well, Maxine Carter—she's in the Leesburg office, so she knows everything—she told me just yesterday that her husband—he's the Leesburg sheriff, you know—says our police have the case sewn up. Just trying to get that man to trip over his own lies. And," she added, nodding significantly, "he has refused, point-blank, to tell Fielding Booker where he was."

"Ah," said Elsie Resnick softly, then was silent.

"What do you mean by 'Ah,' Elsie?" Doris inquired. Doris Bock was as sensitive to the silences in her shop as she was receptive to the chatter of her customers. "Out with it."

"Nothing. Nothing at all." Elsie shook her head firmly.

"Well, I want to change the subject," Mary Royce interposed. "I want to know who's been snooping in the office of the county clerk. Miss Beane—you don't mean Dewey James?" Mary's deep-set dark eyes twinkled. She could well imagine that sparks would fly in the old Grain Merchants Exchange Building when these two characters went toe to toe.

"Among others. She's forever tramping into my office for this and that. She's a prying old you-know-what, that James woman. I wouldn't trust her as far as I could throw her."

"Oh, really now, Miss Beane," put in Doris Bock, who had a very high regard for Dewey. "You don't think she's been prying, surely. After all, the records in your office are supposed to be public."

Doris knew she was skating on thin ice with this remark; but she owed it to Dewey (who after all came in for a wash and set every two weeks) to show some kind of loyalty.

"*Some people* might not consider it prying, Doris," replied Hilda Beane with feeling. "But decent people would. And I'll tell you—when people come poking around into old Cedric's affairs, that's what I call mean-spirited."

By now Hilda Beane had the full attention of the skeleton forces at the Tidal Wave. (It was early Thursday morning, always a slow time for Doris Bock.) Miss Beane launched into a description of Dewey's researches, concluding with the discovery of the purchase price that Harrison Powell had paid for the old Hastings estate.

"None of her blankety-blank business, that's what I say. So

what if the man wanted to give the young fellow a break? He was a family friend, and it was none of her business.''

"But, Miss Beane—haven't you heard?'' Mary Royce was intrigued. Was it possible that there was a soul in Hamilton who didn't know that Cedric Hastings had been the victim of a con man's scheme? "The man wasn't Harrison Powell at all.''

"Oh, I heard all about that. Still, he was a neighbor, and a member of our community. Elsie Resnick knows all about it—he sang with your little group, right, Elsie?''

Everyone else in the small shop knew full well that there wasn't much love lost between the Music Society members and Clyde Scobey. None of them had appreciated the posthumous revelations of his little game. But Elsie seemed distracted; she was disinclined to argue the point.

"Oh, yes, indeed,'' Elsie agreed. "And no matter what you say about him, he sang like an angel. He had a great gift.''

"There, you see?'' said Hilda Beane triumphantly. But Doris Bock and Mary Royce were interested in the real-estate angle. Mary sat back under her hair dryer and contemplated a way to confirm the facts for her story. Finally she hit on it.

"I guess maybe Mrs. James did go a little far,'' said Mary, turning down the dryer again and winking at Doris. "You know, I think it's the duty of the press to rid our community of irritations like that. Don't you?''

"Absolutely,'' Hilda Beane agreed as Doris Bock daubed at her head with a forbidding-looking goop. "You're doggone right. Why don't you do something, Mary? You're sort of in charge at the *Quill,* after all, since your father died.''

Mary Royce had in fact taken over editorship of the small newspaper long before her father's death, and he had been dead and gone these ten years. What was more, Mary was a good reporter and a careful editor, managing to find stories each week that were neither too boring nor too intrusive. Readership was up, and so was advertising. But she let the remark pass. She would have her revenge of Hilda Beane.

"Good point, Miss Beane,'' replied Mary. "How do you think I should go about it? Wait—I know. We'll stage a reenactment, like they do on those true-crime TV shows. With a headline that goes something like this: 'Do Unto Others: Are You Guilty of Prying?' I'll pose for the pictures myself—but in disguise, of course. And people can phone in their tips. We'll run them the following week.''

"Excellent idea," agreed Hilda Beane. "That way, you won't have to mention any names, but the Guilty Party will know who she is."

And so the plan was formulated. In its execution, however, it was very different.

Mary Royce accompanied Hilda Beane back to her office at the Grain Merchants Exchange Building. There, while the county clerk issued precise instructions as to file cards, numbers, and documents, Mary went through the land records and emerged with precisely the same information that Dewey had found. Then Mary rushed back to her office to write her story; but the article, when the paper hit the streets early the next morning, came as rather a shock to Hilda Beane. Indeed, it was a shock to everyone in town, except for those directly involved.

As the *Quill* hit the stands and mailboxes of Hamilton, Fielding Booker was once again tackling the rector of the Church of the Good Shepherd. Booker, never at ease with Cedric Hastings in the best of times, found himself nearly tongue-tied when it came time to ask him about the sale of the house. But Booker knew he must do it. Thus, on Friday morning, having spent all of the preceding day confirming what he could of Dewey's information, Fielding Booker paid a call at the rectory. This time Sergeant Fenton accompanied him, notebook at the ready.

"Thank you for seeing us, Cedric," Booker began when they were settled in the library.

"Not at all, not at all. Pray tell what I can do for you, Bookie."

Booker cleared his throat heavily. "This isn't easy for me, Cedric. But I am going to have to ask you some questions which you may feel are none of my business. I'd like to ask you, before I begin, to cooperate as fully as you can—put aside whatever feelings you may have, and answer me directly."

"My good man, of course, of course." Cedric Hastings was utterly at his ease. Fielding Booker felt a momentary flicker of doubt: Could Dewey James be wrong in her assumptions? Cedric behaved like a man with nothing to fear. Forge ahead, Booker told himself.

"Cedric, it has come to our attention that there was something altogether unusual in the relationship between you and the dead man."

"Unusual? Ha! I'll say there was. He came here and lived under my roof and dandled my son on his knee, all without telling us his proper name. That's fairly unusual, wouldn't you agree?"

Fenton shifted in his chair and glanced at his captain. Stonewalling? he asked with a look. Encouraged, Booker plowed ahead.

"No, Cedric, that's not what I had in mind. You see, it has, er, come to our attention that the selling price of the house was rather low."

"Oh?" Hastings kept his face impassive.

"And I did think, because of that circumstance, that there might have been something more going on than met the eye. If you know what I mean."

"No, I'm afraid I don't, Bookie."

"Well, we have received further information to the effect that there was a plan afoot to sell the property to Mackenzie Munitions."

"Oh, no, no, no. I squelched that ages ago." Hastings made an impatient, dismissive gesture with his precise, cool-looking fingers. "I told them I wouldn't sell to them no matter what they offered."

"You misunderstand me, Cedric. Clyde Scobey had accepted their offer. One million five, in cash."

Cedric opened his eyes wide and stared at Booker. "Surely you're not serious?"

"I am, indeed, serious." Booker studied the rector closely. Was the surprise genuine? Somehow it seemed a trifle too easy, Booker reflected. "Now, if you don't mind, sir, I'd like you to tell me why you struck such an unusual bargain with Scobey in the first place."

"Oh." Cedric took a deep breath. "It's really rather a private matter," said the clergyman with a glance toward the kitchen. Charlotte and Ben were out, but he expected them back any moment. "And, if you don't mind, I'd prefer to keep it that way."

"Yes, I'm certain you would. However—the office of a policeman carries with it many burdens, Cedric; among them is the burden of confidentiality. I give you my word of honor that anything you tell me here, if it isn't strictly material to bringing this man's murderer to justice, will be held in confidence.''

"Thank you, Bookie, for that speech," Cedric remarked tartly. "I am familiar with such burdens, as a clergyman; and as a clergyman, I am also familiar with the propensity of the human spirit to make mountains out of molehills. Good heavens, man. I know what you're sniffing around about. And I tell you that I won't have it. You may go.''

"Cedric, listen to me."

"I said that you may go. If you please. I have nothing more to say to you on the subject.''

Booker rose. He had no heart for this kind of prying, and he was secretly relieved at the rector's intractability; but he knew he must make one more attempt at friendly persuasion.

Booker gave Hastings a pitying look. "It doesn't pay, Cedric, believe me. You will not be well served by this stubbornness of yours.''

No one in the library had heard the back door open and close. Now Charlotte, carrying Ben, stepped into the library. "Stubborn? Cedric?" she asked with a strained smile all around for the company. She put Ben down on the floor, and the child made a teetering, zigzagging line for his father. Charlotte held out a copy of the *Quill*, hot off the presses. "I have always known that my husband was stubborn, Captain Booker," she remarked in an icy voice. "What I didn't know was that he was addlepated enough to sell his family estate for a hundred dollars. Always the last to know. Isn't that what they say about the wife?''

"Good heavens, Isaiah!" Dewey exclaimed to her dog when she had opened her copy of that week's *Quill*. "Dear me, dear me. What will poor Cedric do?" She shook her head sadly at Isaiah, who was lying, one eye open and the other shut, at her feet on the kitchen floor.

A FAUSTIAN BARGAIN, cried the headline. *Dead Con Man Pulled Wool over Good Rector's Eyes*, shrieked the subhead. Dewey read on, appalled.

Clyde Scobey, the California confidence man who was murdered at the Marshy Point Ducking Club last Saturday, purchased the 32-acre Hastings family estate on Palmer Road for the unusual sum of $100.00. Hilda Beane, the county clerk of Adams County for the town of Hamilton, disclosed the sum to the *Quill* in a statement made yesterday at her office in the Grain Merchants Exchange Building. Miss Beane said that the discovery of the anomalous discounting of the property was initially made by Dewey James, local librarian and sleuth *par excellence*. When pressed, Miss Beane admitted that Mrs. James had unearthed the surprising news early last week, but it was Miss Beane, and not Mrs. James, who broke the story to the press.

It remains to be learned if the police are interested in the real-estate deal, which was made privately by the owner, Cedric Hastings, the rector of the Church of the Good Shepherd.

To date, the police have not charged anyone with the murder, although sources confirm that the police have been speaking with Owen Bennet, tenor soloist of the Hamilton Music Society, who had quarreled with Scobey just a few days before his death and made threats in the presence of witnesses.

At the time of the transaction, Cedric Hastings believed the purchaser of his family estate to be one Harrison Powell, of Gorman's Wood, California. Scobey, the dead man, had impersonated Powell during his brief stay in Hamilton. Powell, the son of a longtime friend of the Hastings family, is currently serving time in a federal penitentiary for dealing in narcotics.

There was a photograph of the Hastings place, looking decrepit but nonetheless worth a great deal more than one hundred dollars. "Going, going, gone!" read the caption. Next to it was a photograph of Beverly Simms ("Failed to Find a Buyer"), the realtor who had unsuccessfully tried to sell the place for Cedric. "If I'd know what his minimum was, I'm sure I could have moved that pile," Beverly Simms was quoted as saying.

Dewey put the paper down and scowled at her dog. "Mary Royce ought to be scolded for this, Isaiah. I am very much afraid she has gone too far. And Bookie will think it was my doing.''

As if to prove her right, the telephone began to ring immediately. ''Oh, dear, Isaiah. Here we go.'' She lifted the receiver. ''Hello?''

''Dewey. Booker here, Fielding Booker.''

''Oh, hello, Bookie.'' Dewey's heart sank. ''I have just seen this dreadful article in the *Quill*.''

''Dewey, I thought I had asked you to keep quiet about this affair.''

''Oh, but I did, Bookie,'' she protested. ''Honestly, I haven't said a word to a soul. You can ask George if you don't trust me.''

''I trust you, Dewey,'' he said, relenting. ''What I'd like to know is who tipped off Mary Royce?''

''I'd like to know that, too,'' replied Dewey firmly. The article had made rather free with her involvement in the discovery. ''She really ought to have checked her facts with me first, you know.''

''Well, then, Dewey. Ahem. I—er, have a little proposition for you.''

''For me?''

''That's right. I want you to get on the horn to Mary Royce, or go down there if you have to, and find out who put her up to this poppycock.''

''Well, Bookie, it's not exactly poppycock. It's the truth, in fact.''

''Yes, yes, but I wanted all this business kept dark. Lord knows we need all the advantage of surprise on our side in this one, Dewey. We just got through with the most uncomfortable scene at the rectory, and I don't want to have to go through that again. What is more, I was hoping that my murderer thought we weren't up to snuff. Now that's done with.''

''I'm sure you'll get your murderer, Bookie,'' responded Dewey, feeling sorry for the man. Any murderer worth his salt, however, would know that Booker wasn't up to snuff. ''One way or another, you'll pull it off. Now. When I have spoken to Mary, what would you like me to do?''

''Report to me.''

''Oh, Bookie—I can't just report to you. In the first place,

Mary will know what's up. And I can't lie to her. She's my friend.''

"Fib a little, Dewey. You are the world's most convincing fibber, when you think it's all in a good cause." He hung up.

"Well, Isaiah," remarked Dewey, "I've been deputized by the great Fielding Booker himself. Will wonders never cease?"

Isaiah wagged his tail.

26

FEELING BOLD AND vindicated, Dewey James climbed in her dusty old station wagon and headed downtown for the *Quill* office. It wouldn't do to phone Mary Royce ahead of time; anyway, Mary was sure to be expecting her. She could hardly think Dewey would allow such a front-page story to go unremarked.

The *Quill* had its offices in a small, modern, three-story building in one of the newer shopping districts of town. In the old days Mary's father had run the paper from his living room floor, pasting it up with glue week after week; but Mary, being rather a forward-looking young woman, had brought the *Quill* first into its own offices and then into the computer age. Dewey rather missed the smell of rubber cement; but she supposed it was easier this way.

When Dewey had been shown into Mary's office, she shut the door firmly.

"Uh-oh," said Mary, half smiling. "Wait—Dewey—before you say a word, just let me tell you what happened."

"All right, then, Mary. You tell me." Dewey plunked herself down firmly in a chrome and leather chair and prepared to give Mary a fair hearing. "Go ahead."

Mary Royce settled herself behind her marble-topped desk and related the story of the morning's discussion at the Tidal Wave. Mary was a good reporter; she omitted nothing—not even the sturdy insult that Hilda Beane had made regarding Doris Bock's nose—and by the end, Dewey was laughing in spite of herself.

"Honestly, Dewey," said Mary, her eyes flashing with amusement. "It was too much. That woman should be locked away."

"Poor Doris." Dewey chuckled—for Dewey knew well that Doris needed Hilda Beane's business.

"She'll go to almost any lengths to use up that blue rinse of hers," agreed Mary, giggling. "But you see—I had to do something. Just to fix that Beane woman's wagon. Don't be angry with me. Besides—it was news."

"Honestly, Mary." But Dewey had to agree that it was news. She had thought as much herself, when she learned about it. "But don't you think you were rather hard on Cedric?"

"Oh, no. You know perfectly well that Cedric doesn't give two hoots for the *Quill*. He never seems to mind what anybody thinks or says about him."

Dewey had to agree with Mary's appraisal of Cedric Hastings's character—he never did care about other people's opinions of him. He was an unusual man, to say the least; he established his own principles in life, and then he lived by them. Dewey wondered how the sudden arrival of Harrison Powell had sat with him. Had the young man threatened Cedric in some way? Would he really be moved to impoverish himself and his family (for that was what it amounted to) to ensure Harrison Powell's silence? The good reverend was certainly a man who liked to live up to his ideals; but whether he would go to such lengths to conceal a fall from grace—or the imputation of such a fall—Dewey was unsure.

"Cedric is difficult to read," Dewey admitted.

"But listen—Dewey—what about the murder? Do you think the two things tie in? The house and the fact that the man was an impostor? Maybe somebody found out before Bookie did. Maybe Cedric . . ." She let her voice trail off.

"I don't know what to think, Mary. Except that we would all do well not to speculate further—not among ourselves, nor in print. Don't you agree?"

"I suppose you have a point, Dewey," Mary conceded, "but I didn't print anything that wasn't verified by an eyewitness. And anyway, I hope this affair will convince that woman to keep her trap shut."

"You may lose a subscriber," Dewey pointed out.

"Oh, she hasn't subscribed in fifteen years. Doesn't approve of women editors, I'm afraid."

And so Dewey departed, feeling satisfied, at least, about the purity of Mary Royce's motives. Nobody could fault her, either, for publishing facts that were a matter of public record. It was jut too bad for the earnest but sluggish detective forces of Hamilton that they could be outwitted and surprised in this way by an even more sluggish weekly regional. But that's the way of the world, Dewey reflected.

Having executed her task for Booker, however, Dewey once again felt an impulse to do a little digging on her own. Mary Royce, in fact, had done Dewey a service, really—for when you came to think of it, the newspaper story had loosed the yoke of silence. Now that the strange business about the Hastings house had been made public, Dewey was discharged from her promise to Booker.

Thus relieved of her obligation, Dewey decided it was time to get to the bottom of the distressing affair at the Marshy Point Ducking Club. Mary Royce, in recounting the scene at the Tidal Wave Beauty Salon, had given her an idea.

"Bookie," said Dewey, seating herself in his small office, "I am come to report."

"Thank you, Dewey." Booker looked up distractedly from some notes he was writing. "What did you discover?"

"Not much, really. That is—well, I suppose I had better tell you what you want to hear. And then I shall tell you what I think. Will that be proper police procedure?"

"Yes, yes, go on." Booker was impatient. "How did Mary Royce find out all that gossip and innuendo?"

"Bookie—for the last time, it wasn't gossip. It was a matter of public record. And she heard it, as it happens, from Hilda Beane."

"Good Lord."

"That's right," agreed Dewey with feeling. "But listen, Bookie—I think that woman knows something. And I believe that you really ought to be looking a little close to home, you know."

"I have heard your theories about that young man, Dewey. And I think they are unfounded. As a matter of fact, even if he was Cedric Hastings's son—which we know he wasn't, since he wasn't even Harrison Powell in the first place—but even if Harrison Powell were Cedric's son, you won't convince me that Cedric Hastings is a murderer. No—Dewey. I'm a professional, and you will just have to trust my instincts this once. I have got my man, rest assured. You will know, soon enough, who it is. All I need to do is crack him.''

Booker leaned back and put his hands behind his head. He was tired; and the scene at the rectory had taken a great deal out of him. But he was more convinced that ever that Owen Bennet had done the murder.

While Booker had been at the rectory, a report had come in from a witness who had seen Bennet's car parked near the Church of St. Michael and All Angels on the morning of the murder. All Angels was less than half a mile from an old dirt track that led through the woods into the grounds of the Marshy Point Ducking Club. The information gave Booker the last little building block he needed to put Owen Bennet away for good.

''We even have proof that our man was in the vicinity at the time of the murder, Dewey.''

''Do you?'' Dewey was interested. Was there a chance she could be wrong?

''Yes—and our witness is one of the altar boys at All Angels. On his way to attend at a baptism. Pretty good handle for a witness, wouldn't you say?'' Booker chuckled. This turn of events had pleased him deeply—because of the boy's evident inherent goodness, and because boys of his age had excellent credibility when it came to identifying cars by make and model. Owen Bennet drove a sporty little two-seater that was the envy of many Hamilton males, young and old. There would be little chance of a reasonable doubt about the matter after the altar boy took the witness stand.

''I'm sure you have very good evidence, Bookie. But you know, there are two unsolved crimes in Hamilton.''

''What on earth are you talking about?'' Honestly, thought Booker. Dewey James was really a poor loser.

''I had forgotten myself, until Tom Campbell reminded me, about the burglary at the church.''

''Ah, yes. The burglary.'' Booker smiled a satisfied smile. ''I have thought about that. It fits, you know, with my theory.''

"Does it?" asked Dewey mildly.

"Yes." Booker sighed heavily. He had gone this far with Dewey James; he might as well let her into his confidence on this last point. "The burglary was a cover-up."

"For what?"

"The theft of the gun. Dewey, now this is utterly confidential information. But I don't want you chasing around, stirring up the town, any more than you already have. So I will tell you. The murder weapon was stolen from the storage area behind the music room."

Remembering her conversation with Bruce Ward, Dewey struggled briefly for an appropriate response. "At the church?" She allowed a look of dawning recognition to cross her features. "Of course! The auction. The murder weapon was Charlotte Hastings's gun—the one she was trying to sell."

Booker nodded. "That's exactly right. The murderer broke into the church and took the gun; the money was taken merely to distract our attention. Julia Boucher told me that she thought she had heard someone moving around in the back of the music room the night after the concert. And—well, I'm naming no names, Dewey, but we both know what happened on the day of the concert. One member of the audience was a little out of hand."

The telephone on Booker's desk rang. He snatched it up. "Booker." He listened, his shoulders tensing with excitement. "Found it, did they?" He sounded delighted. "No, no, don't open it. Don't even touch it. Bring it right in, Machen. Good work, son." He hung up. "That's it. That's the icing on the cake. Fenton!" he roared.

Fenton appeared in the doorway. "Yessir."

"Divers got the shell box, Fenton. Bring in our man."

"Oh, dear," said Dewey. "Bookie, I do wish you'd reconsider just for a moment. Miss Beane—"

"Dewey." Booker's tone was exasperated. "Thank you for your assistance in the little matter of the leak to the press. I am very much relieved to know that you kept your word to me on this matter. And now, if you will excuse me, I have a great deal of paperwork to complete." He glanced at his watch. "Judge Baker will issue the warrant in a matter of minutes, once I finish my report."

"All right, Bookie." She rose to go.

Had Fielding Booker been paying close attention, he might have caught the determination in Dewey's tone. But the excitement of the moment was too much for him. He dismissed her with a wave.

27

"HE's DONE IT, my dear," said George Farnham. "Arrested Bennet—I just had word from Tony Zimmerman, who's going to represent him. I hope to heaven he's got a decent case against that litigious lout. Bennet, I mean, not Tony. Else we'll find ourselves up to our elbows in lawsuits."

It was late afternoon, and Dewey James was at home in her kitchen. After leaving police headquarters, she had paid a quick visit to Hilda Beane. The woman had frozen Dewey out, stubbornly refusing to confirm or deny Mary Royce's report of the conversation at the Tidal Wave. Now Dewey was thinking through once more what Mary had told her and trying to come up with a new approach to take with Booker. But she knew from experience that it was almost impossible to make him let go—even when he'd got hold of the short end of the stick.

Now George Farnham had telephoned to say that Booker had gone ahead with Bennet's arrest. Booker would be impossible to budge; he had dug in his heels.

"Oh, George, what are we going to do? He won't listen to reason, you know. I tried to talk to him—"

"Dewey," George interrupted. "Are you so sure that Bennet isn't guilty?"

"I am fairly sure, George. In fact, I have an idea about where he might have been on Saturday morning."

"Do you?" Disbelief marked George Farnham's tone.

"I do, indeed, George. Now I really must go, before any more terrible mistakes are made."

"What are you going to do?"

"First, I am going to telephone Elsie Resnick. And then I am going to church," replied Dewey firmly and hung up.

Darkness was falling by the time Dewey arrived at the Church of the Good Shepherd. Wishing she had told someone of her intentions, Dewey sat in her car for a moment, thinking things through. She was fairly sure she was right about who had done the murder; but perhaps it would have been wise to ask Booker—or at least George—to come along. She hoped that the murderer would confess; but it would be useful to have a witness. Still—here she was. It was time to test her hypothesis—now or never.

" 'Here I stand,' " she remarked aloud. " 'I cannot do otherwise.' " She got out of the car and headed for the dark church.

As she crossed the parking lot, she could make out the light in Julia Boucher's upstairs office at the back of the parish hall; was the woman still at work? Next to it a light also burned in the music room. In the quiet of the early November evening, a thin sound came down to her; Wally Penberry was playing the piano. He almost never seemed to rest, Dewey reflected.

Dewey climbed the stairs slowly. Wally Penberry was working through a piece of distressing atonality; the chords jangled thinly down the stairwell, rattling Dewey's composure. The stairs were unlighted, and Dewey groped her way through the darkness toward the scant illumination from above.

At the top of the stairs she hesitated. The music room was straight ahead; Julia Boucher's office to the right. Both doors were closed. Dewey pushed open the door to the music room and entered.

Wally Penberry, deep in the throes of composition, didn't even lift his eyes from the score before him. Dewey shut the door quietly.

"Wally?"

He looked up, his eyes full of distraction. "Yes? Oh, hello, Dewey."

"Wally—I need your help."

"Something wrong? Flat tire or something?"

"No. Nothing like that. If you would be so good as to come with me?"

Mystified, Penberry rose from the piano bench and followed Dewey out of the music room, into Julia Boucher's cramped little office.

28

JULIA BOUCHER SAT behind her desk, typing up the weekly parish newsletter. She looked old and shrunken—although the two women were contemporaries, Julia had somehow recently acquired the air of a very old lady. Dewey noted with sadness her crabbed, raw-looking hands and the lines of worry that crisscrossed her face.

"Hello, Dewey," Julia remarked, her surprise evident. "Whatever brings you to church of a Friday evening? Wally?"

"Hello, Julia," said Dewey softly. She gathered her wool coat about her; there was a chill in the office—or a chill in the air. "Julia—I think it is time you talked to someone. Don't you?"

"About what?"

"About the murder of that young man."

"Good gracious, Dewey. Whatever are you talking about?" She glanced at Wally. "I believe the police have solved the murder, Dewey."

"No."

"Well, yes—I hate to contradict people, but Cedric telephoned me not half an hour ago. It's distressing, I know—but Wally will tell you that Owen Bennet was not a stable man."

"What's all this about, Dewey?" asked Penberry. He was showing signs of impatience. "Julia told me all about Cedric's call. It's a terrible blow—I can't think where I'll find a tenor for the *Messiah*."

Julia smiled thinly. "Our Wally has a one-track mind. That's why our concerts always sell out."

"Julia, I don't think that you will let Owen Bennet be punished for a crime he didn't commit."

There was a silence in the little room. Finally Julia spoke.

"No. You're right about that, Dewey. I wouldn't let him be punished if he didn't deserve it."

"We're not talking about his just deserts, Julia. We're talking about a specific crime. You thought everyone had forgotten you, didn't you?"

"I don't know what you mean, Dewey." She waved her hands frantically beside her head, as if to shoo something away—a malignant pest, or a persistent nightmare. "Go away. There is work to be done here."

"Here you sit, Julia, day after day and year after year, holding this church together—and what repayment did you get? Who noticed the hundred kind things you did? You thought that even Cedric had forgotten you, was taking you for granted, didn't you? But, Julia—Hilda Beane noticed you. When you went to her office, the day after the concert, and looked up those records. She noticed how much care you took on Cedric's behalf."

"You must be mad. Wally, she's mad." There was a strange light in Julia Boucher's eyes. "She'll spoil everything. Make her stop."

But Wally, frozen with fascination, merely looked at Dewey.

Suddenly the grim stalemate in the little office was shattered by a loud commotion from the stairwell, and the sound of pounding feet.

"She's not at home," said a loud voice. "Probably still upstairs working."

Dewey recognized the voice; it was Fielding Booker. The three turned as one and looked toward the door in expectation.

Booker and Mike Fenton arrived a few seconds later. Booker's face was a picture as he took in the tableau before him.

"Good heavens, Dewey. What are you doing here? Never mind, don't answer me. We haven't got time for chitchat. Julia—I have come to ask you to give me a statement. Are you busy?"

"No. Not at all, really," replied Julia with an enigmatic smile. "Mrs. James was just about to leave."

Booker turned to his sergeant. "You may as well hear the bad news first, both of you. I have arrested Owen Bennet for the murder of Clyde Scobey."

"Yes, Bookie, they know," put in Dewey. "We were just discussing that very fact." She wheeled on Julia. "Weren't we, Julia? There were three people who knew where the gun was, am I right, Julia?"

"Dewy, I beg of you to keep out of this," retorted Booker. "If you won't cooperate, I shall be forced to ask you to leave."

While Booker spoke, Dewey kept her eyes fixed firmly on Julia's. Wally Penberry seemed to have forgotten his music for the moment; he watched the two women, transfixed. Something about the intensity of their unspoken exchange caught Mike Fenton's interest; he looked from one to the other, and then back at his captain.

"Uh, sir—"

"Get out your notebook, Fenton. Are you ready, Julia?"

Julia Boucher prized her gaze away from Dewey. "Have you come to arrest me, too?" she asked Booker, bewilderment in her gaze.

"Arrest you? No, we need you to give us a statement, that's all. About the shotgun."

"She told you about it, then." Julia nodded her grizzled head toward Dewey. "She told you about it."

"Dewey, what on earth—"

Julia tittered. "Well, I guess that she got here first, after all." She turned to Dewey and thrust forward her hands, fists downward, as though to be cuffed. "Fair is fair, Captain." Her eyes twinkled. "Dewey was here first. But rest assured that I will go quietly."

29

"COME ON, NOW, Dewey. Out with it. I've just about had it with this second sight of yours. Tell us how you knew about Julia Boucher. Or I'll never cook you dinner again."

Dewey and George were seated in the library at the rectory. Charlotte Hastings, looking pale and shocked, was sipping gently at a glass of sherry. George Farnham had made himself a stiff cocktail; after this evening's revelations, he had considered pouring a double.

Cedric Hastings was somewhat subdued, but as usual it was impossible to tell from his manner what he might be feeling. He got up from his armchair and went over to the fish tank, leaning down to peer inside.

"Cedric?" asked Dewey gently.

"By all means, Dewey. I'm fascinated. Please tell us everything." His voice had lost none of its buoyancy. Dewey marveled. Could he really be so little touched by the terrible events of the last few weeks? Julia Boucher had been his friend and helper for forty years—yet he had shown not a single sign of regret upon hearing of her arrest for Clyde Scobey's murder. Cedric Hastings was, most decidedly, an odd duck. She looked at Charlotte and George.

"It's a rather pathetic story, I'm afraid. Are you sure you want to talk about it, Charlotte?"

"Yes. I do, Mrs. James—I must. Cedric doesn't need to talk about things, but I do. Besides, I'm sorry for Clyde Scobey."

"I'm not," interposed George. "I think he had it coming to

181

him. Been a crook since he could walk—probably conned his own mother for practice.''

"A bad start makes a bad finish," agreed Dewey. "Very well, then. You see—Owen Bennet wasn't the only person who knew where the shotgun was kept. Julia knew—she had put away all the items that didn't sell, after the auction. Yet no one considered her seriously as a suspect. I don't think Fielding Booker even questioned her before this evening."

"I didn't know Julia could handle a gun," said George Farnham.

"Of course you did, George," Dewey replied. "You told me she was a crack shot, in her day."

"Oh—so I did, so I did. Guess I forgot about Julia."

"Everyone seemed to forget about Julia," said Dewey sadly with a glance at Cedric.

"Besides," pointed out Charlotte, who was the real sharp-shooter of the bunch, "it didn't take much handling. It's hard to miss a stationary target with a shotgun at a distance of ten yards."

They contemplated this grisly truth in silence for a moment.

"Well, why on earth did Booker pursue Owen Bennet so madly?" asked Charlotte.

"Because he's a bad egg. A likely candidate," Dewey replied. "A violent-tempered man with a grudge. And you can't blame Bookie altogether. Bennet certainly strung him along."

"Sure as heck did," George put in warmly. "Don't forget that he refused to alibi himself. Where do you think he was?"

"Oh, I know where he was," Dewey replied. "I called Elsie Resnick today. She had been sworn to secrecy, but once Owen was arrested she felt it was time to come clean. He had enrolled in the alcoholism counseling program at St. Michael and All Angels. They meet every Saturday from ten-thirty to three."

"That sly dog," said Farnham. "That explains why Booker was hopping mad when I went around there this afternoon. That shell box they found in the river had nothing in it but a bottle of whiskey. Bennet. He's a bad 'un. The town ought to sue him for wasting our time."

"I suppose he liked to have his little joke with Bookie," said Dewey. "And he wanted very much to get back in Wally Penberry's good graces. But Julia apparently told him that he had to shape up, or they wouldn't take him back. So he went out that night and tossed his whiskey over the bridge. It was just too bad that Bookie was on a stakeout.''

''Why did Owen make such a secret of it?'' asked Charlotte.

''Oh, that's no surprise,'' put in Cedric. ''None of us enjoys a public confession of his weaknesses.''

There was a long silence, finally broken by Charlotte.

''Why would she want to murder him, Mrs. James?'' she asked. ''He had done nothing to her. Only to us.''

''Oh—but he had. He had ruined Cedric's dream of the Elder Care House. But that project wasn't only Cedric's dream. She was to have a large part in it.''

Dewey looked at Cedric, who had given up on the fish and returned to his armchair. ''There were a great many people counting on you, Cedric.''

''I hadn't thought about it that way,'' said Cedric, keeping his voice even. ''I hadn't thought about what it might mean to Julia not to have that job.''

''But the deal didn't go through—the sale of the house, I mean,'' said Charlotte. ''Because Harrison Powell wasn't Harrison Powell.''

''That's so,'' Dewey agreed. ''But Julia didn't know that. In fact, she suspected that Harrison Powell was Cedric's own son.''

Charlotte looked at the floor, but Cedric gazed levelly at Dewey. ''She wasn't the only one who thought so, you know,'' he remarked tartly. ''Fielding Booker told me this afternoon, Dewey, that you thought as much yourself.''

''He was wrong about that,'' said Dewey. ''All I told him was that the young stranger had made you anxious. By turning up on your doorstep in such a fashion and threatening you. I was right about that, wasn't I? He decided to blackmail you.''

''Oh, yes,'' Cedric agreed. ''He and I had a long discussion on the subject of his paternity. I thought at first that he had come here in search of the facts—that somehow he had got hold of the wrong end of the business. So I set him straight—I told him that it was impossible.''

''Yet you still made that arrangement about the house, Cedric,'' George Farnham pointed out.

''Yes, I did. It seemed the simplest way to keep him from starting up a wild rumor. More than anything, you see, I wanted to protect Charlotte and Ben from having to live with that kind of whispered scandal. Once it starts, you know, the truth doesn't matter much.''

"No," agreed Dewey. "You're absolutely right about that."

"But, Cedric," said Charlotte, "I would have known it wasn't true. If only you had been willing to talk to me about it.''

"There wasn't anything to talk about, my darling. That chapter in my life was closed."

"'I loved thee, Atthis, once—long, long ago,'" quoted Dewey in a soft voice. "And you kept the dead past clear of all regret—is that right, Cedric?"

He nodded. "Sappho knew about love," he remarked with a thin smile. "Yes. Lucy Powell was a beautiful and a vivacious woman; and I suppose I was a little bit in love with her. But after all, she was married, and married to a friend. One day, shortly before they were to leave Kerangani, Daniel was called away to attend to a dying man in a nearby village. Lucy and I packed a picnic and went up to see the forest elephants on Mount Kitale. It was a glorious afternoon; we shared a bottle of wine and commiserated over their leaving. We were both rather sad that the time in Africa was coming to an end. Then, just as we were heading back to town, she told me that she had fallen in love with me. She asked to stay in Africa with me.''

"Great Scott!" exclaimed George. "Put you in a pickle, eh, Cedric?"

"Yes, indeed. And that is why I never kept up my friendship with her—only with Dan. I don't think she really was in love with me—it was the romance of the place that got to her. But I didn't wish to take the chance." He looked at his wife affectionately. "You should know by now, Charlotte, that I can resist temptation when it comes my way."

"He does make rather a hobby of it, Mrs. James," said Charlotte, beginning to smile for the first time that evening.

"Dewey," said George in a plaintive voice, "I don't understand what made you leap to this fabulous conclusion of yours. Honestly. There wasn't anything to point to Julia."

"There most certainly was, George. There was the gun— which was under her care, in that little room. Nobody even bothered to ask if she had been the one to remove it. There was the fact that she had far and away the strongest motive of anyone involved. And you're forgetting the burglary.''

"The burglary?" asked George.

"At the church—on the night of the concert. Well, obviously the Hammond sisters hadn't skimmed the receipts at the door. Who else was there?''

"But there was a burglar, Dewey," said George. "Julia reported it to the police.''

"Did she?" asked Cedric. "Funny—I told her not to bother.''

"She didn't make the report, Cedric—she sent Wally Penberry.''

"With his head full of Mozart and Brahms," mused George Farnham. "Lot of good that did.''

"Just a second, Mrs. James—do you mean Julia stole money from the church?" asked Charlotte.

"Borrowed it, I'd say," replied Dewey. "My guess is that she tucked it away somewhere—for by the night of the concert, she had made her plan. And the report of a break-in at the church would make it easy for everyone to think that the shotgun had been taken as well. The safe was in the same little room, if I recall correctly.''

"Your memory is correct," said Cedric. His voice had acquired an unaccustomed edge of exhaustion and regret. "If only I had paid closer attention that morning.''

"Oh, I think it was far too late, by then, Cedric. If you will forgive my pointing it out, you had burned all your bridges with Julia by then." She glanced at Charlotte. "Your beautiful and capable wife had supplanted her in your personal life; and with disaster looming for the Elder Care House, you had certainly cut her out of your professional life as well.''

"Good Lord, Dewey, you make it sound as though it were all Cedric's fault," George protested. "He can't be responsible for someone who goes round the bend.''

"No, George," answered Cedric. "I'm not responsible for the unhappiness that overtook Julia. But I should have paid more attention to her. Dewey is right—I burned my bridges." He stared at them blankly for a moment. "Funny thing is, I didn't realize there were bridges to be burned." His eyes cleared and he squared his shoulders. "Ah, well, my darling," he said to Charlotte, extending a hand toward her. "I'm not too old to learn from my mistakes, I hope. From the gods comes the saying, 'Know thyself.' ''

When the touchy Miss Hilda Beane got over her snit, she made a full report to Fielding Booker of Julia Boucher's inquiries at the office of the county clerk, corroborating Dewey's hunch. By this time, of course, the murderer of Clyde Scobey, a.k.a. Harrison Powell, had made an even more full and detailed report, on the strength of which she was detained by the law and tried. Her sentence, when it was handed down, was lenient; there were mitigating factors, not the least of which was the letter of character testimony sent to the court by Bishop Lewis, who golfs every Saturday with Judge Baker.

The Elder Care House was finally established, but not in the small rowhouse in town that Cedric Hastings had wished to buy. The institution, when it was finally opened, occupied the grounds of the old Hastings estate. The house had been fully refurbished, thanks to a generous contribution from Mackenzie Munitions. Old Stewart Mackenzie had taken full advantage of tax regulations in establishing the Mackenzie Foundation for the Care of the Elderly; in the end he even made a little money on the deal. But nobody objected; he had done his bit.

Wally Penberry did eventually allow Owen Bennet to join them again as the tenor soloist in the Music Society; not in time for the *Messiah*, alas, and so they performed the Britten at Christmas, with Wally's harp for accompaniment. Never mind, the Britten was lovely, and a great favorite of Josie's, who served up plum pudding and hard sauce at her preconcert lunch.

The party after the concert, however, was singularly lackluster. Mirabelle Meissen had taken it upon herself to make a strange, schnapps-based parody of Julia's famous punch. The Music Society members toasted her politely, then stole, one by one, to be consoled by Nils Reichart, down at the Seven Locks Tavern. All but Owen Bennet and Elsie Resnick, who went to Elsie's place for a temperate but altogether agreeable party of their own.